"*No God Like the Mother* is as beautiful a̶ Kesha Ajọsẹ-Fisher's words are direct ̶ bedrooms, bathrooms, blood, love, and tears of the women and girls in her stories. I breathed with them. I held my breath. I read all night and wanted more!"

—**Michelle Ruiz Keil**, author of *Summer in the City of Roses*
and *All of Us with Wings*

"Kesha Ajọsẹ-Fisher is a talented new writer who debuts with this impressive short story collection that will touch your soul with stories that are both tender and heartbreaking."

—**Heidi W. Durrow**, *New York Times*-bestselling author
of *The Girl Who Fell From the Sky*

"*No God Like the Mother* is the kind of book my soul craves—these stories are gorgeously rendered, poetic and sure handed, but more than Ajọsẹ-Fisher's abundant talent, there lies on each page the thing that can never be invented or taught, and it is simply this: absolute heart. With a seer's eye, Ajọsẹ-Fisher examines themes of motherhood from angles that feel in equal measure compelling, startling, and downright beautiful."

—**Chelsea Bieker**, author of *Godshot* and *Heartbroke*

"*No God Like the Mother* is the sort of story collection that comes along very rarely—honest, precise and meticulous in its emotional and physical detail. These globe-spanning stories—so often set at the intersection of nurture and abandonment, of intimacy and great emptying distance—are each a pristine act of storytelling, an immersion. Kesha Ajọsẹ-Fisher is a brilliant new talent, and *No God Like the Mother* the beginning of an equally brilliant literary career."

—**Omar El Akkad**, author of *What Strange Paradise*,
winner of the Giller Prize, and *American War*

"Kesha Ajose-Fisher's *No God Like the Mother* is a beautiful and moving short story collection about struggle and family, loss and hope. Fisher takes us around the world and into the minds of a number of characters, brilliantly capturing what it feels like to be alive in today's cultural climate."

—**Brandon Hobson**, author of *The Removed* and
Where the Dead Sit Talking, a National Book Award Finalist

"Fierce, protective, despondent, and redemptive, *No God Like the Mother* catapults the maternal figure into the binaries of ferocity and tenderness."

—**Jennie Englund**, author of *Taylor Before and After,*
an Oregon Book Award winner

NO
GOD
LIKE THE
MOTHER

Kesha Ajọṣẹ-Fisher

stories

FOREST AVENUE PRESS
Portland, Oregon

Second edition, 2023
Edited by Andrew Durkin | Inkwater Press
Cover by Gigi Little | Forest Avenue Press
Cover artwork by Omo'Dara Ajọṣẹ Fisher
Interior design by Laura Stanfill | Forest Avenue Press

This is a work of fiction. The events described here are imaginary. The settings and characters are fictitious or used in a fictitious manner and do not represent specific places or living or dead people. Any resemblance is entirely coincidental.

Library of Congress Cataloging-in-Publication Data

Names: Ajọṣẹ-Fisher, Kesha, 1977- author.
Title: No god like the mother : stories / Kesha Ajọṣẹ-Fisher.
Description: Portland, Oregon : Forest Avenue Press, [2023] | Summary:
    "Winner of the Oregon Book Award for Fiction. Kesha Ajose-Fisher's No
    God like the Mother follows characters in transition, through
    tribulation and hope. Set around the world--the bustling streets of
    Lagos, the arid gardens beside the Red Sea, an apartment in Paris, and
    the rain-washed suburbs of the Pacific Northwest--this collection of
    nine stories is a masterful exploration of life's uncertainty"--
    Provided by publisher.
Identifiers: LCCN 2022050469 (print) | LCCN 2022050470 (ebook) | ISBN
    9781942436553 (paperback) | ISBN 9781942436560 (epub)
Subjects: LCGFT: Short stories.
Classification: LCC PS3601.J64 N6 2023 (print) | LCC PS3601.J64 (ebook) |
    DDC 813/.6--dc23/eng/20221130
LC record available at https://lccn.loc.gov/2022050469
LC ebook record available at https://lccn.loc.gov/2022050470

Printed in the United States
1 2 3 4 5 6 7 8 9

Forest Avenue Press
PO Box 80134
Portland, OR 97280

Misery won't touch you gentle.
It always leaves its thumbprints on you;
sometimes it leaves them for others to see,
sometimes for nobody but you to know of.

—*Edwidge Danticat*

NO GOD LIKE THE MOTHER

CONTENTS

NO GOD LIKE THE MOTHER

"COME CLOSE, KEEP WARM."

Mama whispered through Papa's snoring as it hummed high and low behind the curtain. With her back pressed against the wall of our hut, she pulled me into her bosom. Her breath lifted the hairs behind my ear. The rumble in the clouds gave birth to rain and Mama said it reminded her of the day I was born.

"All my children came with the rain," she said. "This one will, too." Her voice was feather-light. She looked down at her protruding belly. "Even the ones fighting to stay inside have no choice when the sky opens." She held up three fingers. "I walked to the tents by myself, three times, and never came home with my children." Shifting on her bottom, she continued: "1960, independence for Nigeria, a sweet year, even here in Ile Omi. I heard of a new midwife across the river. When I tried to cross, the river threw me this way and that. I kept moving and singing to chase the pain away. I sang about birds hiding from rain, and inside, you kicked and kicked. When I mentioned the birds returning after the rain to steal fattened worms, you were quiet."

She poked my side and I could hear her smile.

Mama said, "You were tired from dancing. I sang about the corn I planted and the yams that would arrive in time with your teeth, and you did not move. I sang about sunshine, honey on bread, and still, nothing. I sang about the sweetness of laughter when it comes from deep down, and you started dancing again. I knew then you would stay. The midwife, Iya'agba, and two other women carried me from the river to the tent."

"Were you afraid, Mama?"

"*Ah*, for two days, I cried until my strength finished. That coarse Iya'agba smacked my thighs every time they went limp. 'Open wide, open wide,' she would say, while her women sang into my ears to keep me from drifting off with the pain. With my last power, I screamed. Iya'agba shouted, 'Its head is out!' And there you were in my arms, my girl, with no hair, a big mouth and a smile. That is why I named you *Ayomide*—my happiness arrives. I whispered your name into your ears first, you know?"

"Why, Mama?" I asked looking up at her.

"So you will always be mine."

I smiled. She kissed the tip of my nose and I leaned back against her chest.

She continued, "After erasing your smile with a firm slap against your hide, Iya'agba claimed your beauty was missing. I told her it was not true. She tilted you this way and that like a rag. 'How is this girl darker than both her parents? Her eyes are so tight. There is no height coming to these little legs.' They all laughed."

My head slung low. Mama lifted my chin, and palmed my face. "Keep your head high," she said, poring over me with that look of perpetual exhaustion. "That midwife was wrong, Ayomide. Olorun carved a smile right into your face—how can He be wrong?"

I ran my fingers across my lips. "Mama, why did Olorun do that?"

A burst of excitement left her body as she cheered, "*Adupe, o.*" Music scuttled through her skin whenever she spoke about God.

"Yoruba people say Olorun, the keeper of the sky, watches everything we do. He is all that is good. He gave you the gift of joy so you can spread happiness, and you have done so every day of the nine years since you came to us. Seek Him when life is hard but especially when life is sweet, *so gbo*?"

"Yes, Mama. I hear."

Papa stirred in his sleep. Mama held a finger to her lips. She whispered, "I do not want to wake him before finishing this story."

The smile she tacked onto her words urged me deeper into her embrace. My scrawny elbow caught her in the ribs. "Careful," she said.

"*E pele*, Mama," I apologized.

"Before you came, Papa said Ile Omi was cursed, and we were cursed. I told him we should leave this village and go to Lagos where curses cannot reach any person. He agreed. But after seeing that you survived, he kissed my feet, praised me as if I had performed a miracle. Then, he ran around Ile Omi, pouring palm wine down his throat. That *amuti* emptied a full gourd by himself. He sang about his new child as if he was the first to have one—imagine the surprise when the villagers heard he celebrated that way over a daughter. He even announced you at the chief's compound—bare-chested, slapping the ground, daring anyone, anything from this life or the next to touch him. Some people say he should not have taunted the spirits that way, but I know it was happiness and not ghosts that chased him into the forest over that hole."

I gasped at the thought of Papa falling. "Papa broke his legs because of me?"

"No, *o*." Mama chuckled. "Papa broke his legs because he drinks too much."

Thinking of Papa as he slept behind the curtain, I tried to imagine him with speed in his steps. The picture would not come. To me, he would always be slow and portly, with contorted legs and a white beard that added more years than he had lived. I wished I had known Papa when palm wine and joy drove him to run around the village.

A kiss to my ear drew me from my thoughts. "After Papa saw you thriving, he planted orange seeds. 'As long as this tree lives, so will Ayomide,' he said. He believed it to be true. Soon, you were crawling, and he crawled with you. When you stood, he did too. The first time you walked, he took you to your tree and said, 'The abandoned cannot prosper.'"

Mama paused for a breath. "I knew then we would never leave Ile Omi. We saw all over the village farms yielding yams in excess. Fish jumped out of the river into our bellies. Mangoes rained on our heads. Babies stayed. Papa decided the curse was removed. Soon, I was in front of Iya'agba again.

"Iya'agba—Elder Mother, they call her, but to me she is the woman who takes. From me, she has taken plenty. She told me that screaming during childbirth calls spirits to suck life out of the new. She said, 'Take your time healing. Do not return to the work of cooking. No cleaning or meeting your man too quickly.' No wonder she does not have a husband who will stay with her and all those children. No one knows or dares to ask which oils she uses in her ointments. She could be a witch, I told him, but Papa said spirits fear Iya'agba, and I must return to her."

Mama rested with a heavy sigh. I looked on silently. She inhaled and exhaled, and her chest hummed near my head. I felt her tears land on the back of my neck as she coolly described holding a son fresh from her womb the year after me. She had placed a hand on his chest, feeling it rise and fall with haste, until it slowed, and then stilled. She paused and stared ahead before speaking of a daughter, who came the year after him.

She went on.

"Iya'agba said, 'Olorun punishes when one takes before He is ready to give,' meaning the grief from losing a son was why Papa rushed me to have another. But God would not punish by giving sick children, I told her, and certainly not a child with two heads, one alive and the other ... *oku*. No one wanted to touch it, not even me. I cried and cried. It cried and cried. Iya'agba decided, 'The bush, then.'"

I turned to see my mother's face glowing in the lantern's light. A brittle grin covered her sorrow. I pinched her on the wrist and kissed her cheek. "Mama, I take your pain and give you sweet."

She dropped her tearful face inside her palms. "They say children must be born perfect, Ayomide. What that means, I do not know. I suppose for a child to be perfect, it must have two arms, two legs, ten fingers and ten toes, a working heart, one head, and two parents? *Ah*, I should have left this place long ago.

"I told Papa that the devil was seizing its chance. I begged him, begged him, 'Please—take me to Lagos. Anywhere but here.' But he said Nigerians were fighting. The cities were dangerous. Biafra this, Biafra that."

"Mama, let us go to Lagos now, now," I begged.

She laughed heartily. Papa raised his head to the racket. He lifted the corner of the curtain to see our shadows cast against the wall at a time of night when the village had grown still.

He grumbled, "You know I am trying to sleep, now?" His white beard was matted to his face.

I lied flat and watched my mother rise off the floor. She stood in the doorway. Papa was silent. Mama craned her neck to the sound of rain drifting across the roof. Papa and I awaited her next move. She hissed in pain, nearly keeling while clutching her abdomen. After steadying herself with a few breaths, she extended her hand towards me. "Ayomide, come."

Papa strained his words. "Where are you going?"

She did not look at him. Her face remained calm as still water.

"To the birthing tents. All my children come with the rain."

((● ●))

I SQUEEZED HER HAND as we waded through the river's currents. Mama paused when the pain stiffened her. She spoke through gritted teeth. "Pull me." I did. She thrust herself forward. I sang about birds, and worms, and yams, and corn, and honey on bread. She laughed from deep down.

The straw caps of the tents appeared through the woods before us. A spark darted above the trees, and the sky roared a deafening reply. Mama looked up and muttered, "Spirits."

Just as she buckled, two young women ran out to carry her in.

"Wait outside," one of them told me.

The rain slowed. I wiped water from my face and peeked around the curtain. The fabric emitted an odor of burnt sage. Mama screamed. A kerosene lantern splattered the women's shadows onto the walls. I watched the shapes of their bodies move from canine-like, to tree-like, to round—like sheathed spirits fighting to escape the dark.

"Go away," I snarled, with a clap.

Inside the tent, on hands and knees, Mama rocked back and forth, mumbling to soak up the pain. Louder, I shouted at the spirits, "Go."

The rain stopped.

Draped in black from head to feet, Iya'agba slunk past me. After peeling the outer fabric off her body, she raised her wrapper across her chest and tied it before kneeling at my mother's feet. Two plaits dangled past Iya'agba's shoulders. She tied them up in a scarf and touched Mama's thigh. Mama screamed louder than before.

"Do not touch me, *o*," Mama spat. "Witch."

The other women begged for calm, "*E ni suru*, Mama Ayomide."

My mother kicked at Iya'agba. The other women held Mama's feet and controlled her arms.

"Calm down," Iya'agba commanded. "*Ehn*. The baby does not like this kind thing, *o*. Thank God your husband told me you were coming here. Did you go through the river?"

I stepped across the threshold to provide answers. "Yes. *Beni, mah. A fi okunbo.*"

Without turning from Mama, Iya'agba snapped her fingers. "*Bosita.*"

I immediately went back outside to wait in the sodden midnight air. I heard whispers.

"Too much blood," Iya'agba said, just before one of the women scurried out with an empty pail.

Each time my mother squealed, I felt empty. The quiet would come and fill me again, and back and forth it went. A raspy cry finally replaced the peace. I peered in and saw Iya'agba place the baby's wriggling body on Mama's abdomen. My smile blossomed. I had heard that babies were born blind, but my brother slithered up to Mama's chest to find his food.

Mama sang, "My son," as her head fell back in exhaustion.

Iya'agba tallied his features. "He will be tall."

Mama smiled.

"Eating like that, he will be strong."

Mama attempted a chuckle.

"His skin is dark as—" Iya'agba stopped. "Something is wrong."

I rushed into the room. Iya'agba handed my brother to one of the other women. Mama's arms spread out at her sides. Steps away from reaching the silence surrounding her, I froze. I wanted to do something, anything—free my limbs, scream, shake my mother loose from the thing that seized her. But I could only watch in that fixed state. The midwife tapped Mama on the chin.

"Open your eyes. Open your eyes." She poured water on her scalp and smacked her cheek.

The woman standing beside me swayed as my brother wailed in her arms. "Ayomide, wait outside."

I sat on the stoop outside of the tent, bowed my head, and clasped my hands. God was silent. The women were mumbling before Iya'agba came to the doorway with her hands coated in my mother's blood. I nodded and let my hands fall to my sides. She smiled and I was struck by her beauty. She did not resemble the witch my mother had spoken of. Her sharp cheekbones hid beneath skin smooth as the stones beside the river. Her dimpled smile hung above ample breasts—like a childless woman's, though she was the mother of eight. Standing without her wrap, she appeared soft, womanly, safe.

The woman who had left to fetch water returned with a full

bucket and placed it at the midwife's feet. I watched Iya'agba immerse her hands in the water without speaking a word to me. They passed whispers to one another. The musty smell of sage faded. The empty pails clanged. The silence collapsed inside my brother's cry. Iya'agba finally named my mother *oku*. "How could my mother be dead?" I wanted to ask. The other women covered her body with a cloth, and their faces fell, and their words reverberated in unison above my mother.

I pushed the curtain aside. "What happened to Mama?"

All three women raised their eyes. The world spun around me. Two arms entered my haze and swept me close. I heard screaming that sounded too distant to be my own, though it was. I heard a woman's voice, "Ayo, calm down." Her grip tightened around me.

"Free me," I shouted, as I tore at her face, blouse, and wrapper.

"*Ni suru*," she begged, but I had no room for patience.

"Mama! Mama!" I cried.

Iya'agba came near. Cloaked in black once again, she placed a hand on the shoulder of the woman who held me. The woman loosened her grip. I fell to the ground.

"Sit up," Iya'agba ordered. "And follow me."

The two of us moved to stand above Mama. Iya'agba prayed. I knelt beside my mother and lifted her hand to my mouth. When I opened my eyes, the lantern was out. Iya'agba was gone and the shadows had left with her.

When I emerged, she was sitting on the stoop with my swaddled brother asleep in her arms.

"Ayomide," she said. "It is time to go."

"Mama *nko*?" I asked.

"We will take care of her. *Ma* worry."

Steadily, we walked away from the tents. I kept turning my head, waiting for Mama to catch up to us. The midwife veered off the path into the bush. I stepped along, scraping the sloshed terrain with my bare feet, fearful of my brother's fate as he slumbered in the folds of that cloth. Wedged in the space between my brother's life and Mama's death, I knew a great task fell upon me.

Seeing the pallor of dawn gradually infect the sky, I begged, "*Ejo, ema pa.*" Iya'agba paused. I stopped too, heavy with fear.

"What makes you think I am going to kill him?"

I hid my hands in the sweaty pits of my arms, and dropped my gaze. "We are going into the bush, mah."

Iya'agba lifted my chin. I saw only her eyes.

"Small girl. At only nine years old? What you must have heard about me." She pointed West. "The river flooded the way. Unless you prefer to swim?"

The tightness around my collar slackened. I fiddled with the wet hem of my dress and almost smiled as we took to the trail.

Iya'agba bid my father a somber good morning. "Papa, *eku aro, o.*"

With a hand over her heart, she shook her head from side to side. Papa nodded and stared at the bawling baby that had replaced his wife. His massive hands would not rise to accept his son. He pivoted on his cane and turned his back to the midwife. She rocked the baby silent and handed him to me. "I will be back to feed him."

As Iya'agba was leaving, she murmured something about Papa having too much love for one woman. I sat on the floor and held my brother firmly in the bend of my arms. He squirmed and stretched and yawned. His hands reminded me of chicken feet as they lingered near his fleshy mouth. I kissed the tip of his nose. Papa stared blankly at the wall.

Iya'agba returned with two of her young sons trailing her. They came in rowdily, startling my brother. She hushed his cries with the tip of her breast.

"There are rules," she said. "If you men followed them, I would not have to take in so many children."

Papa stared at the wall.

I thought the baby would be smothered beneath all that skin

but I only looked on. As my brother's silence finally settled the room, I tapped my foot to the rhythm of his gulping. Iya'agba hummed her own tune before speaking to Papa. "I will feed him until he no longer needs milk. We can talk arrangements later."

Papa bowed his head.

Tears ran down my cheeks. Iya'agba said, "Do not cry, Ayomide. Death is also another part of life. Olorun knows what He is doing."

I nodded.

After the feeding, she asked, "Who wants to hold him?"

Papa sat down beside me with eyes like ruptured tomatoes and reached for his son. When Iya'agba and her boys left, I scooted closer to my father. He wrapped his free arm around me. "Ayomide," he said. "There is no God like the mother, *so gbo*?"

I smiled.

"Now, what should we name him?"

I whispered into my brother's ears, "Your name is Tokunbo."

SLEEP

I HAVEN'T SLEPT IN years. I've forgotten what it is like to lay my head down and be lulled to sleep by the presence of night. I scuffle with the sheets, searching for the perfect cocoon. I hum, I wait, I count sheep. Sleep evades my body until chasing it exhausts me. I stare at the clock, the moon, and the clock again. Even with the sky's slow effort, it gives birth to dawn. I rise out of bed. My bones scream at me, "Lie back down." I know I must get up. Stretching reminds me that rigor mortis happens only to the dead—but when I hear my children darting down the hall toward my room, I know I am still alive.

The two of them throw themselves at me and press kisses into my skin. We all fall back onto my bed. It hurts. My boy crawls on top of me and I catch his elbow between my ribs. It hurts more than when he pokes my eyes asking if I am awake. The girl is quieter than usual. She sits at the foot of the bed lost in thought. She knows that Mommy likes hushed mornings. Her greeting is short and without notice, she leaves the room. I stay there with my boy's limbs wrapped around me. He warms my neck with his breath as I collect the details of his dream: the Legos, assembled as soldiers, had risen from the pile in a wooden box. They battled with the stuffed animals on his bed and collaborated to take him prisoner. He was strapped to the bedpost by his hands and feet, and he begged for his freedom.

"I was so scared, Mommy," he says.

I ruffle his hair and kiss his cheek. "I have bad dreams too."

He offers to show me the Lego men still surrounding his bed, and then drags me out of my room and toward the battlefield where plastic corpses line his floor. The maze of toys and fluff-filled animals do not tell the story of any recent commotion, as I see it. But he describes each fighter from his dream with unbridled enthusiasm and intricate detail.

"See, and I got away, Mommy."

"I'm glad, love," I say. "Get dressed, the school bus will be here soon." I step over a copy of *Gulliver's Travels* on my way out.

I connect my phone to the speakers. The soft music blends with our voices at breakfast. I hand the husband his coffee with more cream than he likes, and he pauses to let his hand grace mine. His embrace is strong enough to break me, though I know he intends the opposite. He stares into my eyes longer than usual. "Make it a great day," he says. His blue eyes are surrounded by red and his lips tremble as he presses them to mine. I nod after the kiss and look away. He tosses those same words over his shoulder again as he walks out of the house.

I add whiskey to my mug of coffee, believing no one is looking. My son wags his finger. I wink at him. The first sip is warm and awakens the flow of blood in my veins. I feel again. I step into the pantry with the bottle and swallow two more gulps. My bones quiet. I invite the children to dance with me when Sia sings, *I don't need dollar bills to have fun tonight*. Only my boy enters my ring of excitement. We swing our bodies to the music. After, we climb into our jackets and hike through the moist autumn morning to wait for the school bus.

The adults, mostly fathers, huddle with their morning mugs,

and I hang mine at my side. The two women there ask each other questions about their children, feigning interest with choreographed nods and smiles. I do not engage. The men confer about the copious leaves fallen upon their yards, and how raking ate away their weekend. "At least you have a quiet house for a few hours to rest," one says to another. A third nods. "I'm happy to be kid-free any day." He looks at me quickly, then to the ground.

I see the girl leaning against the trunk of a pine tree. My boy runs circles around her until he falls to his knees. He rises covered in mud, and I step out of the cluster of parents.

"Now you're all dirty," I say, as I wipe his legs. He fights through the help and my mug falls near my feet. I look up to see if anyone noticed. I'm relieved to find them engrossed in petting each other's dogs. My son is startled by his mistake, eyeing me nervously.

"It's okay. We just have to be careful, huh?"

The girl nods.

He scuttles away from me when the bus appears. Parents wave to their children. I blow kisses. I walk slowly behind the crowd to avoid being pulled into a conversation, especially one that might expose the liquor on my breath.

Back inside, the silence is freeing. I belt my apron and begin to tidy up from breakfast. Pieces of pancake are scattered across the floor. My son's milk cup is full. I turn on the television for background noise and begin collecting dishes from the table. I shrug at the topic on Portland's local news and turn to CNN. The anchor has invited a panel to discuss current events. One woman attempts to emphasize her point by shouting at others. I stare at the screen for a few moments and decide I need to sit instead. While my body is alerted I intend to rest, my bones remind me I cannot. It will take two pain pills and double the Xanax chased with Jameson to quiet them down. I feel ready to feel better. I sit and wait.

This is when my day truly begins. My muscles pull away from my joints and my blood loosens. The aching itches for a way out, and I scratch every inch of skin to help. I lie on the floor and stretch in front of the roaring fireplace, until I am warm through my core. I talk back to the television when an advertisement warns of impending doom should the wrong candidate become president. "How can anyone still not see her as the better option?" I say, and I compile my disdain into a line for my Facebook page. I crawl over to the coffee table, sit up and open my laptop. Politics tends to brew anger in people, I know, but I feel awake, certain that my opinion might sway the confused among us. My first thought takes a peaceful approach in hopes of appealing to my like-minded followers, but I am stirred with fury, blurred by what feels real to only me. I stare at my computer screen.

What is on your mind? Facebook asks.

At first, I think today is the day I will finally convince John Zemke to change his mind about his politics. But no. I don't want to engage in another online fight—not today. I close my laptop and fight my way up the stairs. I sit in a warm bath until the water turns frigid and my fingertips wrinkle. I air-dry on the tiled floor. Rubbing lotion into my limbs steadies the flow of blood inside me, but I know the stiffness will return soon. I head off the pain with one more pill. The air softens, noises abate, breathing is easy. I should eat, but food will only slow the opiates. I lie back in bed and sink into that place where immense relief eats away time.

A couple of hours slip by. I return downstairs and empty the Jameson bottle. I know I must replace it before the husband gets home. He'll want to talk about it, among other things.

The cashier at the liquor store still cards me even though I sear my face into her memory each time I come in. A while back, I screamed at her, "How many black women live in this neighborhood or even come in here?" She had shrugged. Once, I pulled off my beanie to expose the gray braids scattered across my scalp. Another time, I offered to show her my stretch marks. Today, I place my card on the counter next to the bottle and avoid her eyes. She smiles and says, "Thanks, Mrs. Gathers."

Beside the counter is the newspaper rack. On the front page

of *The Oregonian* is a picture of my family. I pay for the bottle and walk, head down, toward the exit. When I look up, the customers are staring at me.

"What?" I yell, before running to my car.

At home, I am safe inside my silent freedom again. I measure out a cup of whiskey and tuck the bottle into its slot on the bar. I sit and sip through more journalists arguing. The pictures on the screen move in waves until my family's photos are splattered up there, too. I turn it off and close my eyes.

I hear the vultures squawking at my front door. I don't feel myself walking, let alone twisting the latch. The noise, the cameras, the bombardment of inquiries force my eyes open.

"Mrs. Gathers, KATU news, how are you faring today?"

"Mrs. Gathers, Fox 12, can we talk to you?"

"Mrs. Gathers, our condolences on the second anniversary of your …"

I slam the door shut and make my way over to the couch. I hide inside a throw. The phone rings. It is the husband. "Marley, I'm on my way home."

"Don't," I say, but I know the request is futile. He will arrive shortly and smell the drink on me. He will want to talk about it, among other things.

I drag through the push and pull of vacuuming and wince in pain as I finish washing the breakfast dishes. The slog up the stairs consumes the rest of my strength. I crawl to a halt outside my boy's bedroom door. I sit in the doorway wondering where to start. It is foggy inside my head again. I curl into a ball. I cannot bring myself to stand. My bones will not unravel. Only my tears move.

I hear the front door unlock—the scavengers squeal at the husband too.

"Marley?" he calls out, once he's safely inside.

I want him to be anywhere else.

When he finds me in a fetal position on the floor, he says, "I shouldn't have left you today."

"I am fine."

"Marley, you don't look fine."

I swipe my hand at him. "Leave me alone."

He sits beside me, rubs my shoulder. "Were you watching the news?"

I nod. "Politics."

He sighs, "I thought we said the television would not come on today, and you would ignore the reporters outside."

"I didn't talk to them. And I didn't watch TV for that stuff."

He lifts my chin. His brow wrinkles to the fragrance wafting from my lips. "It's noon, Mar."

"I had one drink."

"Meds?"

"You know I couldn't sleep. Just a couple of—"

He stands suddenly, places both hands on his head. "You cannot go on like this. I cannot go on like this."

"*You* can't go on like this?"

He cries, "You can't become this zombie."

Furious enough to spit, I stand positioned for a fight. "You cannot become this uncaring."

His face loses all color and I know I have struck a nerve.

"You have to get better. You just have to. Dr. Grayson said—"

"Dr. Grayson wasn't there!"

"Okay," he says.

I can see his ripened frustration. His huffing grows more bizarre. I feel heat emanating from him as he pushes past me into the bedroom. He empties the contents of the laundry basket onto the floor.

"What are you doing?" I yell.

"Cleaning up. I should have done this long ago."

"Do not touch his things. He likes his room like this."

"It is not *his* room."

I watch as he shatters the soldiers with his feet, scattering their limbs in pieces. He gathers and pours them into the hamper, entombing them with stuffed animals. Then, he jams the copy of *Gulliver's Travels* inside like a sordid headstone.

"Stop it," I shout, and reach for the hamper. We scuffle for it until both of us land on the bed. A heavy maple syrup scent is woven into the sheets. The husband releases the hamper, shoves me off him and rises with sweat on his brow. His hands rest on his hips, and he stills his breath. I steady mine in silence, covered in Legos. I see him pick up a book, *the* book—my son's favorite book. He bares his teeth, attempting to rip it in two. Defeated by the thick binding or loss of will, he tosses it to the ground. It lands with Gulliver's bound body facing us. The husband stares piteously at me. I can see in his eyes he knows I am broken.

As I am restoring the trophies on the shelf, he says, "This isn't us, Mar."

I do not take my eyes off my work. "Then what is us?"

"What about your daughter? Want her to see you like this?"

"What about your son?"

"Mar, he's gone."

"Shut up."

"Mar, he's not here, and I'm scared I'm going to lose you too."

"I said, stop it."

From behind me, his embrace is tight.

"You're all arms today," I say, before breaking his hold.

He begs, "Please, let's go see Dr. Grayson."

"No."

"We booked an appointment for this reason. Come on."

"So she can tell me I'm crazy?"

"No one thinks you're crazy."

My hands go up. "He was your son too, why aren't you angry?"

"I am angry, but I can't let it wreck me. Please, for the sake of our family, let's go see Dr. Grayson."

I continue digging in the hamper, and feel the Legos between my fingers. I pull out the tank and place it on the floor. The husband watches as I recreate the battlefield that sends my son running into my bed each morning.

He says soothingly, "Please, Marley, just one visit."

I look up, and he kneels. His palm cradles my chin. "Hey."

"What's one visit going to do—waste of time really."

"Please?"

"Just one?"

He nods.

I rest my forehead on his chest and sigh. "Okay."

IT'S NEARLY SEVEN IN the evening. The sitter arrives shortly after the last of the reporters pack up to leave. I pull myself together and throw on a black dress that the husband finds dour. We drive, serenaded by the hum of the engine. I know he thinks of me as shattered, or near it. I can feel it in his silence. When he hugs me in the mornings, I feel him checking to see if I'm still whole. I hear it in the way he tiptoes around life—around the truth.

Dr. Grayson's office is in a cold room with a grey couch and two beanbags like heaps of snow tucked in each corner. The walls are white, covered with her credentials and posters of quotes from true crazies speaking on what is real and what lives in our minds. She is overweight and Caucasian, and she confidently sports a bald spot with thick glasses. She taps on her clipboard and says in a voice more delicate than I remember, "Welcome."

I sit on the couch beside the husband. She smiles at him. It's hard to breathe in this white room of white furnishings and white people. They sit comfortably in their skin and smile at each other as if they hold the remedy for what ails me. I stare at the floor. It is brown like me, wooden like me, trampled on by others like me. Every cell in my body itches to leave. Dr. Grayson messages him with a wink that says, *I'll fix her this time*. He winks back. The scene is hysterical. I chuckle. They stare at me piteously.

I gaze about the room as they wrap up their small talk. She concludes with how spending the past summer in Ghana had changed her life. The husband nods, smiling as if wholly enthralled by every aspect of her existence. She points at the picture of herself with some children in Accra and says, "They are just the most beautiful kids I have ever seen. They're so happy even with so little."

I nod.

"I like that wooden statue of the woman with a baby on her back," I say.

"Thanks," she replies. "Isn't it cool?"

I shrug.

"Have you ever been to Africa?" she asks.

"No interest," I answer.

"Why? If you don't mind my asking?"

"I just have no interest. I don't know the culture. I don't know that I want to start learning now. I just don't."

She nods. "That's fair, but it's just so rich and life-changing."

I return a nod.

The husband chimes in, "What she means is, she grew up here in Portland. There was never any reason—"

"What *I* mean is, *I* have no interest." I roll my eyes. "And you know what else really bothers me?"

Dr. Grayson sits up. "Please."

"When we are in a restaurant, and I look up from my plate to find everyone gawking at us. I feel like a fucking zoo animal with all those leering eyes. I swear. Is it the interracial thing? What are they looking at? And that was way before my—before this thing happened. Now, I get eyes following me around the grocery store, the mall, all over the place—stupid rubberneckers to my tragedy."

Dr. Grayson says, "So, I find it interesting that you call it 'your tragedy'."

"Who else does it belong to?" I ask. The husband raises his hand.

I throw my head back and stare at the ceiling.

"Marley, don't do that."

"Do what?"

"Shut me out."

Dr. Grayson is silent. He says to her, "Help me out here, Doc."

She straightens her shirt, scoots to the edge of her chair, and dives in to the rescue. "Open dialogue is the best course here, Mrs. Gathers."

I face her stiffly. "We tried other shrinks, you know. One, a white guy, refused to look at me. Another, a black man, glared at me disapprovingly. My husband wouldn't even consider a black female doctor. 'She'll just take your side,' he said. You, Dr. Grayson, are as close to good as we could get."

She shuts her eyes as if I had thrown sand at her face. "I'm not sure how to take that."

I uncross my arms and sit loose in my skin.

She says, "Let's move on, anyhow."

I shrug. "I'm ready."

She asks how I am doing. I wonder why she does not want to know how *we* are doing.

"I'm fine. Ask him."

He pulls my hand into his lap and begins, "I love my wife. The incident is wreaking havoc on her and I fear I am going to lose her completely."

"It's always my fault," I say, leaving my hand where he holds it captive.

"That's not what I am saying."

Dr. Grayson interjects, "What do you think is happening, Mrs. Gathers?"

I move my hands onto my lap, and study the creases on my knuckles. I exhale the breath I feel I have been holding in for two years and say, "My head is full."

"Okay," she answers. "Let's clear some of it up."

"Well," I begin. The husband kneads my shoulder as if preparing me for a fight in the ring. I move slightly beyond his reach. "I want things back the way they used to be."

"What if you can't have that?" the husband asks.

Dr. Grayson speaks, "Please, let her finish."

"I want a lot of things. I want to rewind time. I want to live in a place where people I consider good friends don't deliver their condolences via text message. I want neighbors who don't act as if my loss is contagious. I want to stop getting misspelled Facebook messages. *Sorry for your lost*, they say. As if my tragedy—sorry, *our tragedy*—is too much of an interruption to their day to fucking proofread. I don't know, I want to have wings to fly out of this room. I want to see the future." My shoulders slump. "I want to sleep."

"You're still not sleeping?" Dr. Grayson asks.

"I lie down, but my mind is always running. Sometimes, I am at that park, and I see my boy playing, laughing, happy. He was so sweet, so small."

Dr. Grayson hands me a box of tissues. I don't feel the tears. I can't feel anything. Inside of me, that ability has been replaced by a gaping hole.

"Mrs. Gathers, can you please tell me what happened at that park?"

The husband shakes his head.

She chides him, daintily. "I need to hear her tell me."

I was wrong. Dr. Grayson is the one who wants to talk about it, not the husband.

"I was distracted by work," I begin again. "To escape it, I fell into a discussion on Facebook about some bullshit. The children were playing on the playground. They were occupied. After I told that Zemke guy where to shove it, I looked up from my phone. I didn't see my boy where I had left him. His sister was hanging from the monkey bars. He had been in the sandbox. I called his name, 'Luke.' He didn't answer. I yelled for him. He was quiet. Some of the other mothers yelled too, but he wouldn't come out. That park is so big and he was so small.

"Still, I had hope. It had only been seconds. 'Stop every car,' I shouted, but all I saw were people corralling their own children and leaving. Those mothers shielded their children from the madwoman who had lost hers. 'Please help, my son is missing,' I kept yelling, but when the cops came, they restrained me. 'Ma'am, calm down.' My son was stolen and they wanted me to calm down."

I realize I've been screaming.

I breathe in and out. "Then, reality blared at me, 'Your son is gone.'"

There is now redness in the husband's eyes, and then profuse tears. For the first time, he weeps in front of me. For the first time, I hold him, so he doesn't break. I wipe his cheeks. "I am so sorry. I am so sorry," I say. "I lost our boy."

I go on, crying too. "He would have been six this year. I haven't slept since he was taken, Dr. Grayson. My days begin the same. Luke drags me out of bed. We go to his room. We talk, read, stare at the sky. In those moments, I feel clearest about everything. After breakfast, I notice he has left his milk untouched, and then the haze returns. So, I drink, to rush the day. Sleep or no sleep, I know when the morning comes, so will my son."

"Mrs. Gathers, you miss your son. Let's help you deal with your loss in a healthy way, so you can feel whole again."

"I don't want to feel whole," I yell. "I want my baby back."

The husband taps my knee.

Dr. Grayson says, "I understand."

"I'm so sick of everyone telling me to carry on as if they can't see it hurts every part of my being just to breathe."

"Okay, Mrs. Gathers, tell me how the rest of your day is."

He chimes in. "Pills and the alcohol."

I know he can feel me glaring at him.

"Have you been mixing substances?" she asks.

"Oh God, here we go. You probably need caffeine to wake up. He runs to start his day, but I can't get out of bed without feeling like I'm on fire."

"Are you also taking Xanax?"

I fold my arms across my chest. "As prescribed."

"Do you take anything besides what we've mentioned today?"

I shrug.

"Do you see your son when you're not dreaming?"

I shrug again.

"So, our goal is to get you to a place where you don't need these things. The Xanax should help you sleep, but please don't mix it with alcohol and certainly not opioids or anything a doctor hasn't confirmed as safe."

I nod. "I know."

She winks at him, triumphant for the day at least. He nods to agree. That look of victory in the husband's eyes is to blame for my explosion. I rise from the couch. "Can we go now?" It is not a question.

The husband roars. "Marley! Sit down."

I sit.

"You don't care anyway," I say, swiping at air.

His hands go up in supplication. "Marley, please. What do you think I've been going through? I couldn't just stop living. I had to carry on, we have bills—a mortgage, cars, medicals, children—one child now. You've been able to stay back and hide your sorrows behind drugs and alcohol and walls that I kept intact for you, while I carried on, dragging my pain from day to day out in the open."

I stop him. "He didn't live inside you, he lived inside me. He wasn't stolen from you; he was stolen from me."

"Goddamnit, Marley, he was stolen from us! I lost him too. I miss him too." His tone cools. "We cannot have our son back, but we can be as present as possible for our daughter. That happens only if we change focus. You don't feel supported by some of our friends and family? That's okay—fuck them. But what about the people who called, sent flowers, cards? What about the women in the neighborhood who brought meals, cleaned, took care of our daughter when you couldn't? What about your sister flying in just to sit with you in silence? What about me? The love you want to fill that void resides only in our son, I know, but the love you need is here in our daughter, in me."

"Can we take it one day at a time to start?" Dr. Grayson asks.

He nods. I nod.

"Okay. We have gone past an hour. Next week, same time?"

I grip my husband's hand. "Yes."

MY DAUGHTER IS ALREADY in bed when we relieve the sitter. I glide into the darkness around her and slip my body beside hers. She stirs.

"Hi, Mommy."

"Hi, my lovely girl."

She huddles close. Her breath is slow and steady. She places her head next to mine. Silent for a moment, she then says, "Today was the day Luke was kidnapped?"

I pull closer. "Yes."

She sniffles. "I miss him."

"Me too."

I sit up.

She asks, "Do you think they'll ever find him and bring him home?"

"I hope."

She wraps around me from behind. "I can tell you're still sad."

"I am." I cry. "I love you both with all my heart."

My hands on hers, I howl from deep, deep inside of me. She does not let go. Together, we sob, loud enough to feel lost together. The husband knocks on the door. We go quiet. I say, "We're okay." His shadow vanishes from the base of the door.

My daughter and I remain bound as one until she speaks. "This morning, after breakfast, Luke asked me to play Legos with him."

I turn to face her. "He did?"

She nods. "While you were dancing, we shared my pancakes in his room."

I kiss her forehead.

She continues, "He told me he'll come back again tomorrow."

"Yeah?"

"Yes. You wanna come?"

I nod and say, "I wouldn't miss it."

Just as the doctor prescribed, I take my pills. I lie in bed and wait. Next morning, my bones are quiet. I rise out of bed with ease. The sun spreads its arms across the auburn forest outside my window. My son is beside me. He leads me to his room. There, my daughter waits. I read *Gulliver's Travels* to my children and watch as they play with Legos for as long as they want.

THE SILENCE BETWEEN US

THE DAY KAREEM WAS born, I was already yawning inside my mother's arms. He would take his mother's milk and hear her coo into the folds of his ears. Fatima said his name, "Kareem," and still swears that he smiled from hearing it. I would not hear my own name until my mother died and my father cried out, "Emilola, I'll name her after you."

Kareem was not my brother, but I called him that when the words came to me. He named me Sister though he already had two. Life became a daily unearthing of lessons derived from running and falling and laughing and hiding in the fields in my father's compound. It was there, beneath my orange tree, on a quiet, sunny afternoon that I discovered my first loose tooth. I opened my mouth, and Kareem peered in.

"See," I said, as I pushed the tooth to and fro, until it came out. Kareem glanced away when blood swelled and spilled through the hole in my mouth. Cradling the tooth in my palm, I said, "Look at it." He covered his eyes.

"*Mumu, wo*," I ordered. He lowered his hand. Together, we marveled at the stone-like nugget surrounded by red.

"Yours will come out today or tomorrow," I promised, digging into the ground.

Kareem fingered each one of his teeth. "None of them are soft."

"Don't worry, Kareem. We were born on the same day. Your mum said we walked and talked at the same time. We are both six. Yours will fall soon." I buried my tooth with dirt while Kareem looked over my shoulder. He seemed sad that it happened to me first. I wanted him happy again, and I wanted to be the one to make him so. Before I lifted that rock, I pictured a different ending. After I dropped the rock against his mouth, I wanted only for him to stop screaming.

I told Fatima, "He just started crying when I turned around."

Fatima gasped with a hand over her mouth and quickly picked up her son. "Kareem, move your hand," she pleaded. "Let me see." When he lowered his hands, her eyes widened and she gasped.

I shouted, "Kareem, what did you do?"

He wept, "I am sorry."

I kept my hands atop my head, shaking as if still in shock.

He glanced at me, then away. "I hurt my own self, Mama."

Fatima carried him to my bathroom and stripped him naked inside the tub. As the water ran, she caught handfuls of it and rushed it to his mouth, one after the other, begging for his silence, "Shh. Shh." As long as Fatima had been our housemaid, I had never seen her moved by panic. When she carried Kareem out in a towel, she spat, "Emi, bring his clothes."

I flinched and stared at his soiled clothing strewn about on the floor. Instead of touching the bloody clothes, I used a hanger to drag them closer to the tub. I left the bathroom when I heard a scream from the parlor.

Kareem's thirteen-year-old twin sisters fawned over him worse than his mother, as if they had birthed him themselves. All the while, Kareem was crying on Daddy's sofa with a bath towel around his body and a smaller one pressed against his wound. He cried until sleep silenced him.

Upon his waking, Fatima fed him fish broth, one spoonful at

a time, and sent the girls to buy ice-cream. When Daddy returned from work, no one scattered at his presence as they usually did. He kept our hug short to tend to Kareem, and Fatima.

Years later, just after Kareem and I turned eleven, the two of us were sitting under my orange tree. I asked if he remembered that day. He raised a hand to the scar on his top lip. "Yes—now."

Our eyes paused on one another. I asked, "Did you tell anyone?"

"Tell anyone what?"

"What happened. Don't you remember?"

His smile lifted the scar, and his dimples appeared. "I remember sitting in the back of your daddy's car."

"That is all you remember?"

"No. I remember my mama was crying in the front seat, and you were staring out of the window next to me. Then your daddy turned on the radio and my mama stopped crying and the full moon followed us all the way to the hospital. It was the best day of my life."

"The best day of your life?"

He nodded and pointed to the sky to persuade me of his statement's truth. "*Olorun*. It was."

I shook my head at Kareem and looked down at Daddy's crossword puzzle in my lap.

"My wedding day will be the best day of my life," I said.

He sat closer to me as I sang about white gowns and presents and six slaughtered cows and how sad it was that getting married was as far into the future as flying cars. Chimaka, our gardener's brute of a son came over. "Are you two keeping secrets?"

I snapped. "No!"

He said to Kareem, "Come and see my sword."

By "sword," he meant a stupid stick, but Kareem rose off the ground with joy, keen to follow. He did not heed my glare urging him to stay. They ran circles around me, chuckling about nonsensical things as they knocked their sticks together. Chimaka twirled his branch above his head and kept calling it a sword, pronouncing the silent W. Kareem saw me seething, and laughed. Angered, I blurted out, "It is pronounced *sord*: S-O-R-D."

They stared at me as if trapped inside my words. It was always like that with the help's children whenever I corrected their English. They would just glare at me as if dazed. I often pictured them babbling in vernacular as they ran about the yard, playing through their days and mocking me while I was forced behind a desk in a classroom. A week earlier, I had come home from school to find the seat of my swing broken. I asked Kareem and he shrugged. None of the others wanted to admit to breaking it either, even when Daddy lined them up and threatened to sack their parents.

"Who broke this thing?" he asked, with his left eye twitching.

Standing beside Daddy I added in pidgin, "*Na* who break am?"

They all kept their eyes to the floor. The silence continued. I saw Daddy remove his belt. "Two lashes each, then."

Standing before Halima, one of Kareem's twin sisters, Daddy ordered her to turn around. Kareem's hand went up, "I did it, sah." Halima stepped back in line. Kareem took two lashes plus two more for making Daddy wait. Later, when I asked Kareem for the truth, he shrugged and said, "It is in the past."

I started inviting Kareem to read with me at bedtime after that. He listened intently, and expressed astonishment—as if the words blossomed right off the pages before him. He was a good listener— unlike Chimaka, whose mind wandered off to places that caused him to shout angrily when confusion set in. I detested Chimaka, and his abhorrence for me was palpable. On the afternoon of his swordfight with Kareem, as I filled in the boxes of my puzzle in the shade of my orange tree, Chimaka dug acutely into me, repeating himself: "Suh-ward, suh-ward, suh-ward."

Kareem laughed.

I gathered my books, and dragged the shame behind me in a huff. When I reached the top of the stairs, I was alone. Over the balcony, I saw a strange transition taking place below. Kareem and Chimaka were spinning hand in hand, leaving space between them and me. I wanted to scream—but when my mouth opened, nothing came.

Inside the house, I was met by the cloudy aroma of boiling chicken stew. I went into the kitchen where Kareem's mother, Fatima, stirred the pot in sync with her sluggish humming. She tightened the yellow scarf around her head and said, "Emilola, come in. Have you finished playing with Kareem?"

I did not respond.

She spoke softly. "Emi, have you finished playing with Kareem?"

Stone-silent, I stared at the refrigerator for a moment and opened the door. My flask of water was shoved near the back. I grew frustrated trying to grab it. When Fatima repeated her question again, I snapped. "*Ah ahn*! Leave me alone. I don't play with Kareem anymore."

Fatima turned around to see my face. "What happened?"

I drank my water and repeated, "I will never play with Kareem again!"

"What happened, my dear?" she begged, her expression awash with panic.

She called me *dear* as if I belonged to her. Her hands on my shoulders, she pored over me with the same languid eyes he had. Her calmness was another quality he shared, and it tore right through me. I had the power to sever the torture of her serenity, I knew, and the longer she cut into me with Kareem's eyes, the more she fueled my indignation.

"Don't touch me," I spat, smacking her hand before I knew what I had done. Heat moved through my body. Fatima's eyes watered. I wished to go back in time, to moments earlier, maybe even the few steps before I entered the kitchen. But I landed on the day she handed me a bottle while Kareem ate from the warmth of her bosom. Each time I climbed onto her lap and lifted her blouse, she would gently fold my hands away. I used to say, "Mama," because I heard Kareem say it, and it pained me profoundly when she kissed my cheek one day and said, "No, call me Auntie Fatima."

Now she was touching me and calling me *dear*. Fatima was staring at me inside my father's kitchen, knowing she was not my mother, making me feel it more than I ever had. Losing care of my tongue, I shouted, "Kareem should respect me, you know?"

Fatima's bow implied she'd heard something worse. "I will make sure of it," she replied.

I guzzled my water, and threw the emptied flask on the counter. Fatima flinched. My heart felt like it plunged into my stomach. The words *I am sorry* would have easily reversed her tears and eased the twinge in my gut, but Kareem's twin sisters spilled noisily into the kitchen, singing about the busy marketplace. Eighteen years old and still pint-sized, they resembled a pair of dolls in their matching yellow *saris* and finished each other's sentences as if they had rehearsed it.

"Obalende market is too much for me, *o*," said Halima, as she unraveled the fabric around her head.

"Too much, *o*," added Safiya.

Halima planted herself in front of the standing fan and her words whirred through the slats: "And the bus kept taking more and more passengers."

Safiya chimed in, "More and more passengers."

After greeting their mother with pecks on each of her cheeks, they began unraveling nylon bags, tossing yams and plantains into bins, opening and slamming cupboard doors. Halima gushed about a grocery store she had seen in a movie.

"There was meat—clean, no blood anywhere."

I coughed when it seemed the twins would carry on that way forever.

They turned to me. As if sharing a mouth, they asked, "Emi, Kareem is not with you?"

"Why should he be with me?" I barked, with my palms spread wide. "Am I his mother?"

Each girl glanced over at Fatima, whose eyes were locked onto the simmering pot of stew. When they turned back in my direction, I felt as if time was slowly inching by. They responded in unison, "Sorry, Emilola."

Now, three of them kept their eyes locked on the linoleum floor. The air stiffened and my body steeled itself. All I wanted was for someone to speak, or shout, or just tell me why losing Kareem made it so difficult to breathe.

In the evening, Daddy and I sat at the table eating rice smothered in chicken stew. He lifted a glass of water to his mouth. The liquid sieved through his mustache before reaching his lips. I licked meat off a drumstick and hurriedly gathered rice into my mouth. Displeased by the scraping against the plate or the way I used my fingers to help the rice onto the spoon, Daddy said, "Slow down, now. Where are your manners?"

"But rice keeps falling off my fork," I yelled.

"Watch your tone!" He pointed his doughy index finger at me. "And, use a knife as well. Nonsense."

I stared at the bushy curls amassed at his knuckles and nodded. He did not see me roll my eyes.

"You really should know how to use a knife and fork when food is in front of you, you know?"

"Yes, Daddy."

He tilted his head and placed eyes on me. "What is wrong with my sweet, happy girl?"

"Nothing, Daddy," I said, evading his look.

His heavy hand was suddenly on top of mine. "My darling Emilola, what is the matter?"

I knew speaking my truth would send Daddy into a fit, and I found that side of him despicable, unless he was defending me. Kareem once told me that Daddy caught his former driver stealing money from his briefcase. He said he heard my father dragging the man around our compound. Sometimes, Kareem embellished the truth, but he was no liar. When he said Daddy forced mud into his driver's mouth, I found that hard to believe. But when he added that Daddy stood above the driver and yelled, "Don't ever take what is mine," that I believed. He hated thieves. Kareem further described Daddy ripping off the man's clothes, and chasing him away in the nude. While Daddy had done things one could consider strange, I could not fathom him making a man walk naked through that part of Ikoyi, scaring all the new white neighbors.

Daddy drummed his fingers against the table. "Emilola, stop daydreaming and tell me what the matter is."

"I don't want to go to school in America," I whispered.

He rose suddenly out of his seat and dropped his fork on the plate. The crash from metal against glass drew Fatima from the kitchen covered in suds at the knees. "*Oga, wetin* happen, sah?" she cried.

Daddy shouted, "I am speaking to my daughter."

Fatima bowed.

His tone subsided. "Go out, please."

Fatima backed out.

He sighed and turned to me. "Now, what is this nonsense about you don't want to go to school in the States?"

I eyed the sweat crawling down his neck. His eyebrows bunched to meet in the middle of his forehead. When logic should have stilled my tongue, panic loosened my lips. I used the firmest voice I possessed. "I am not moving away!"

"*Sharrap*," he yelled.

I crossed my arms. "All my friends from my primary school are heading to Holy Child. Why do I have to go to another country for secondary school? It's stupid!"

Then I saw the man from Kareem's tale. The sting of his rage remained on my cheek well into the night. When I saw his shadow hanging behind the curtain on my bedroom door, I shouted, "Go away. I hate you."

BREAKFAST WAS QUIET. DADDY took tea without condensed milk and hardly touched his food. I stared at the egg swimming in a layer of palm oil on his plate, hoping he would break the yolk with the edge of his toast. Had he done so, I would have called it disgusting, and pretended to want to vomit—and he would laugh. Instead, he threw his napkin on the table, called for the driver and left without saying goodbye.

Kareem's lanky body was crouched at the base of the stairwell when I came down. I hurried past him as if he blended with the air. He followed my full-bodied walk, trailing behind like a duckling. Without stopping, I hollered, "Why are you following me?"

"I always walk you to your school," he replied.

"I thought you were busy playing with your new best friend, Chimaka?"

"He's not."

"Well," I said with a shrug. "You tell him everything though?"

"I don't."

"He is a foolish boy. I wouldn't trust him with my secrets."

Kareem was silent.

"I just wish he would go away," I said.

Kareem shouted, "Me too."

I stopped and turned around. "Why? Did he do something to you, too?"

"Doesn't matter. It's in the past," Kareem said.

I wagged my finger at him. "You should tell your mum."

He shook his head. "It is no problem."

"I can tell her for you. What did he do?"

He shrugged. "Nothing." When he smiled, the scar pulled his lip askew.

"Okay," I said, as I turned around. "I think I want to walk alone."

"Emi—then please let me carry your bag," he offered. "It looks heavy today."

"Do you promise to tell your mum?"

He nodded.

When my bag hung on his left shoulder, his right hand reached for mine. We smiled every time our eyes met. As we walked, a rabid dog in a disoriented haze wandered near the roundabout. We veered away from it. "That thing is still alive?" I asked.

Kareem chuckled. "I heard it bit Chimaka, that's why he is a wild animal."

"Yes," I concurred. "Chimaka is a wild animal."

We ran hand in hand as if headed safely into a future set solely for two. We did not stop laughing until we reached the gates of my school. I accepted my bag from him and crossed from the dirty pockmarked street through the gates and onto the manicured lawn of the schoolyard. When I turned to wave, his wink assured me that the only thing between us was time.

As CERTAIN AS HEAT accompanies the sun, Kareem was outside waiting for me when school was over. We strolled home hand in hand, through the ebb and flow of crowds, sharing how the day had been.

"I told my mama about Chimaka."

"Good job," I sang, and I hugged him.

"She said she will fix it, no *wahala*."

"I told you," I said, smiling as we separated.

At my father's house, Kareem held open the door for me. I told him to come back to play in an hour. He nodded, smiled, and walked away.

Halima and Safiya hummed as they watered the houseplants. From Daddy's desk, I asked, "Isn't that Kareem's job?" They shrugged.

Later, when Fatima delivered my supper, she was overly animated about how delicious her stewed beans were—touching her fingers to her lips and letting her eyes roll inside her skull. Kareem usually brought my meals to my room unless I was dining with Daddy. When I asked about him, Fatima left without responding. I waited for Kareem to tap on my door so I could read with him at bedtime, but awakened hours later to Daddy shaking my ankles.

"Emi, darling. Wake up." A bag of Butter Mint sweets dangled near my face.

I sat up. "Thank you, Daddy."

He kissed my hand. "I am sorry I struck you."

I nodded.

He took my hand. "Listen. The reason I want you to go to America is because you have aunts and cousins who can teach you woman things."

I sighed. "But I have Fatima and the twins. And Kareem."

"But America can give you opportunities you won't have here in Nigeria."

"But what if I'm not happy?"

"When you're successful, you'll be happy."

I wanted to ask, *What about the people I love*? But I knew I was out of excuses that Daddy would understand, so I said, "Okay."

"I love you, Emilola. You'll see."

I pulled the blanket over myself. "I love you too, Daddy."

Kareem was not waiting to walk me to school, and an eerie silence floated about the compound. I quietly followed behind some other students with my head down. At school, during morning assembly, I stood in line with my mind adrift. Could Kareem be angry with me, or had he simply vanished into the night? I did not understand why he had neither returned to play as I had requested nor come to finish our book. The headmistress' mention of my name hauled me back into the moment before everyone bowed to pray. The rest of the morning was abuzz with praise on my father's head for being fortunate enough to send me to America. My teacher, Mrs. Ezekwe, allowed my classmates to linger around my desk. They all wanted to know which American foods I would try first, and threw out the ones they knew of:

"Magdonas?"

"Kentucky Fried Chicken?"

"Buhgah King?"

Kayode wanted me to send him a pizza. Lekon requested a bicycle. Shola wanted nail polish and fashion magazines. Aisatu asked me to send her snow. Before I could ask her why, someone called her foolish and said it would melt traveling all the way from New York to Nigeria. Mrs. Ezekwe played Majek Fashek's *Send*

Down the Rain before the closing bell. To top that strange day, the teachers took turns wrapping their arms around me like I was one of their children, and the headmistress laid a wet kiss on my cheek. After recalling it all to Fatima, she said I was blessed to have received all that attention. I never mentioned that Kareem had not walked with me before or after school.

Daddy's driver arrived early on Saturday morning to take me to the airport. Fatima and the twins sang me praises in unison. They cursed the devil, begged for God's mercy, and wished me success, happiness, and health. I wanted to ask about Kareem, but after the way I shouted at all three of them for bringing him up just days earlier, I was not surprised by their forbearance. I climbed into the back seat of the car, and Daddy joined me. He gave me an envelope filled with money, and said, "Work hard and be a good person."

I stared at the road ahead.

MY FATHER'S HOUSE NOW stood with a slight lean. After twenty years, my orange tree's branches sagged like an old woman's arms, but the tree itself still maintained its prominence in the field. On the front steps, someone with a head of patchy white curls ambled toward me. The woman suddenly released her wrapper into the breeze and screamed, "Emilola!"

The taut skin on her face did not match the wrinkled hands that grabbed mine. "Auntie Fatima," I sang, as her crooked posture wrapped tightly around me. She squeezed out a short prayer. After we split, I introduced her to my husband. "This is Professor Matthew Edwards."

She replaced the hood of her *sari* and said to him, "You are welcome." She bent to greet my son, Tobi. He clung to my knees at her approach. When she pinched his cheeks, he screamed, "No!"

I said, "He is just tired. Twenty-two hours traveling with a two-year-old was too much for all of us."

Daddy hugged me before shaking hands with my man. They

were carbon copies of one another—short, lean, and bald, with thick spectacles.

"A professor of African American studies, I hear? Very impressive," said Daddy.

"Thank you, sir," Matthew replied. "I have wanted to make this trip all my life."

"I suppose wishes come true then."

He nodded. "Yes, sir. Yes, they do."

Daddy lifted Tobi in the air, and the boy laughed. Matthew and I shared a look of astonishment at hearing our son chuckle with such purpose. With Tobi on his hip, Daddy invited Matthew to join him in his office. I heard Matthew say as they walked off, "I hope a month is long enough for me to learn a little Yoruba, sir."

Daddy patted Matthew on the shoulder, "I will make sure of it. No problem."

Matthew said, "You mean no *wahala*?"

Daddy laughed. "Yes, yes. You are well ahead."

I hooked Fatima's elbow and she led me into the house. She had cooked rice, *egusi* stew with smoked goat meat, and fried plantains, she said—all in one breath. I drank in the aroma and kept it close. The thickness of heavy spices in the air along with the scent of pending rain reminded me that I was indeed back home.

I walked around the house. Tile had replaced the old shag carpet. The green on the walls, once vibrant as fresh banana leaves, was now pale from scouring. The dining-room table held countless engravings from Daddy losing his temper, and its mahogany burnish had dulled, but it remained sturdy in the bay window facing the backyard. Outside, the playground of my childhood had been razed, and the beginnings of a brick structure sprouted in its place. No swing set, no field, and no signs of the help or their children.

I invited Fatima to join us at the table for supper. She glanced over at Daddy. He nodded. She carefully pulled out a seat beside him. She fidgeted, resting her elbows on the table while her body slumped and straightened repeatedly. Finally, she decided to pray in her most taxing English, and ended with, "In Jesus name, we pray."

Settling in the tranquility of her prayer, she doled out food. When Matthew raised his hand, I imagined him criticizing her English—*It should be in Jesus's name we pray*. I was relieved when he asked her, "Aren't you Muslim?"

Fatima looked over at Daddy.

"She was," answered Daddy, "but she has been a Christian since she has been with me, *ehm*, us."

"And you all speak Yoruba, sir?"

"Yes. Fatima speaks Hausa too. Hausa and Yoruba are different tribes, but only one God watches over all of us, as far as I am concerned."

"Do you also speak Hausa, Emi?"

"Not as much as I do Yoruba."

Matthew added, "So, how long have you been their housegirl?"

I looked up and saw Daddy and Fatima both staring at Matthew.

I chuckled. "Matt, try some food."

He bit into a piece of goat meat. "This is delicious, Fatima." He nudged me. "How do you say *this is good* in Yoruba?"

"*O dun*," I replied.

Matthew raised his fork and voice, "Oh *doon*."

We all laughed. Fatima asked Matthew, "Emi don't cook dis?"

"Emilola likes eating more than cooking," he replied, before emitting his lethargic laugh into the air.

This new laugh seemed to have sprouted legs now, but it was when the plane landed that I first noticed it. I felt as if he created it just for coming to Nigeria. I heard it used again with the customs officer, and as we exited the airport, when he threw his arms in the air and shouted, "Africa, I'm home!" For the duration of the drive, I watched my serious husband turn aloof with the driver, and I hoped he would soon go back to being that pensive professor who had climbed into the plane with my son and me.

I slapped his knee beneath my father's table.

"What?" he gasped. "I'm just kidding."

"I do cook, just not this well."

I lifted a mound of rice with my fork into my mouth and chewed, counting to fifty in my head.

Matthew snickered, followed by that newly fashioned laugh. He pretended to chew his food in an exaggerated manner. The table wobbled from my pinch on his thigh.

"What now?" he said. "The silent counting is just hilarious."

"Not to me, Matt. We talked about this."

He raised his voice slightly. "No joking allowed on vacation."

"Rude, dude." I pushed back my chair.

Matthew threw his hands up. "Oh, here we go."

I snapped, "Stop it, Matthew."

"Oh, now we're fighting on my first night in Africa?"

The way he stretched the word—*Af-ree-kah*—made my stomach churn. I held back the scream lodged in my throat, shrugged, and pulled closer to the table. I calmly stated, "Who's fighting? I just don't want to be insulted in front of my family."

There was more silence—too much of it to feel like a celebration. After ten minutes of my subdued chewing and Daddy and Fatima quietly passing glances back and forth, Matthew finally broke the peace with another question. "So, is it true that Nigerians call African Americans *Akata*?"

Daddy coughed out his drink.

"What does it mean exactly?" Matthew added. "I've heard it translated as cotton picker. Is that correct?"

Daddy coughed again. Fatima fanned him.

I nudged my husband. "Don't be crass."

Matthew raised his water glass. He sipped it and added, "I have also heard it linked to *nigger*—is that correct?"

I looked at Daddy, who seemed to be shrinking further into his seat.

"Daddy doesn't want to talk about that, Matthew." I stiffened my brow and whispered, "And it doesn't mean *nigger*."

Matthew laughed. "We're just having a conversation here, Ems."

"No," I spat. "You're shoving your insecurities down people's throats."

My husband turned to me. "Honey, stop getting so worked up."

I looked at Daddy. He dropped his gaze over his plate of food. Fatima stood frozen. Daddy said, "Ah, Fatima, did you make something sweet?"

"We have cake. Tobi will like this cake I bought from Shoprite."

Hearing his name mentioned along with the word *cake*, Tobi looked up from where he was playing with his toy cars on the floor. "Cake?"

Matthew prodded me in the ribs. "Hey, you can have cake. As long as you chew every bite like a hundred times right, honey?"

His laugh—slow and wheezy as it rose through his chest—fell out of his mouth in chunks. I got up and left the table. Matthew came after me. The shouting between us lasted for more than an hour. I refused to leave our room or show my face to anyone that night, and slept with Tobi by my side.

A HARSH RUMBLE FROM the generator rattled near my window. The gateman's voice carried equally as loud. My nightgown clung to my skin. With electricity restored, I stared at the fan, awaiting its start. It groaned back to life, slowly gaining momentum, and at full force, only stirred the cloying air. I pulled the curtains apart. In daylight, the outside was muted, and covered in dust. I finally pried open the window, permitting sooty Lagos air into my room. When the gateman shouted, "Good *morrin'*, mah," I waved and shut the window.

Fatima had bathed and dressed my son, and changed his diaper twice. We sat before a meal of fried eggs and boiled yams, without anyone mentioning my chewing, *akata*, or niggers. Tobi ate mango slices out of Fatima's hands, and trailed her to and from the kitchen as if a bond had formed between them in the night. Matthew had left early to tour Lagos with Daddy's driver, Fatima told me. I said I felt ill and returned to bed. There, I stared at the wall of cupboards until my eyelids grew heavy. Four hours later, I awoke to Fatima's singing and Tobi giggling around the house. Matthew entered the room, "You up, Ems?"

His embrace came with the scent of the homemade oils he had encountered from the mullahs we saw on the drive into the neighborhood. "I hope you chose only one scent," I said.

"Of course, I did not." He chuckled as he nudged my chin. "How's my girl?"

"Fine now." I took him by the elbow. "I'm sorry, Matt."

"For what?"

"Our stupid fight last night."

Confusion wrinkled the skin around his eyes. "You do seem more easily annoyed since we got here. Is it close to your monthly visits?"

I closed my eyes, took a deep breath and said, "You know what? It's nothing."

"Hey, look at this, Ems," Matthew said, after clawing eagerly through a nylon bag. "A man carved this mask with his very own hands from wood that grew right out of pure Nigerian earth. Only ten thousand naira. How cool is that?"

"Very cool, babe," I replied, with a shrug. "Did you at least haggle with him?"

"Now, see, that is an American solution to African problems. Would you haggle for a dress at Barney's? Nope."

"Okay, Matt. Not today," I said. "Can you at least relieve Fatima and take over with Tobi? I need to sleep."

"Sure. I'm too wired to sleep, and you can't get enough of it. Jet lag just affects everyone differently, I guess."

"You'll crash soon, I'm sure."

"But not yet. Ha!" he said as he kissed my cheek.

The next day, Matthew wanted to go to The New Afrika Shrine to see Femi Kuti perform. Like a boisterous puppy, he hopped about. "This isn't just any club, Ems. Fela's own offspring is performing live. I wish you weren't too sick to go."

"I *am* too sick."

"Oh, honey. You sure you don't wanna go? Drinks, good food, dancing, music…"

"I am sure," I answered, to break the monotony of his words trailing into my head. "Have a great time tonight, honey. I need to rest."

After hiding for most of the next day, I crawled out of bed and slogged around the house. Inside the kitchen, music from the radio swirled in the air. Fatima hummed while her frail hands dragged a mop back and forth.

Pressed in the doorway, I said, "Daddy should get someone else to do all this work."

She kept her eyes on the floor. "Why? I am still here, now."

"After thirty years in this house, when do you rest?"

Fatima chuckled, "*Walai*! You sound like true Americana. I will rest when I am dead."

I grabbed an apron. "Then this American will help you clean."

"No, no—please. I don't need help."

"I am helping," I declared. Fatima flinched, nodded, and threw her gaze to the floor. I softened my tone. "I rested enough while you took care of my son. Please, let me help."

Fatima slapped my hand and grabbed the apron. "Go, relax in the bed. If I need help, I will call. Pounded yam and okra soup for supper. I will fry chips for Tobi."

"Okay. I can help with cooking too. Just let me know, please."

She shook her head and laughed. "You have been gone too long."

I stood in the doorway between the kitchen and the dining room, pondering the best way to liberate my thoughts. "How are the twins?" I muttered.

"What?"

I repeated the question.

Fatima answered succinctly, "Married with children."

"And, um …" My tongue was heavy. "Have you heard from—have you heard from them lately?"

"They visit once a month. You just missed them."

I scooted closer to the refrigerator. "And what about—Chimaka, the gardener's son?"

"Oh, he has been gone a long time. Everybody left except me." Fatima got off her knees and lifted the pail. Her eyes at a slant, she smirked. "Anything else?"

"No," I said. "*Kosi.*"

I WOKE UP AT noon on a rainy Friday, three weeks into our stay. Fatima came into my room with a tray of catfish pepper soup.

"What hurts?" she inquired, stroking my scalp with shaky hands.

"I'm not pregnant, if that is what Matthew told you. This rain just makes me tired."

"Tell me, Emilola."

Our eyes connected.

I sobbed into my hem and faintly professed, "*Kosi.*"

She hissed. "Don't tell me it is nothing."

I looked up and said, "But I have a husband."

Fatima huffed, and spoke English, "And also you have a heart that is your own one."

I sat up and crossed my legs on top of the concrete-firm bed Daddy bought for my visit. Fatima's hands cradled mine. I eyed the veins woven beneath her skin, still not speaking.

Reverting to Yoruba, she begged, "Tell me," stretching her words in a crisp whisper.

I fingered my wedding ring.

Fatima squeezed my hands. "Now listen, and listen well."

My answer was a wary nod.

"Kareem is getting married."

"That's good news," I said with overstated enthusiasm. "We thank God."

She quenched my excitement. "*Tank* God *ke*?"

"Why?" I asked, wincing as if she had hooked me in the spine with a rod.

"The girl he has chosen is not to my taste. Vanity is her business, but she is ugly." She patted her chest. "Inside here, she is unkind. She speaks ill of others for no reason, and uses money to buy the friends she has—I know. You should have seen her come here one day and turn her nose up at this house. *Shio*! Igbo girl with too much pampering."

I shook my head. "Don't say that."

"On top of that, the wedding place is too far, and I am too old. She even says I must stay in hotel. Imagine that? God forbid."

"Did you tell Daddy? You should be there with your son on his wedding day."

"I don't bother your father with my problems."

I rose with sudden vigor. "That is crazy. I will take you to Kareem's wedding. Where is it?"

"Ikeja. A few hour's drive with go-slow. These days, every car in the city travels all at the same time."

"It is settled."

TOBI WAS EXCITED TO go swimming at The Clubhouse with the men, and none of them would miss my moping around the house, Matthew said.

"Kareem is her only son," I told Matthew. "I cannot let her miss his wedding."

"Of course not."

"Are you sure?" I asked him.

"Yes," he answered, holding my hand. "It'll be good for you, too."

"What does that mean?" I countered, snatching back my hand.

Matthew kissed my forehead.

I said, "We grew up together. We were born on the same day, and did all the same things, you know—it's nothing like you think."

He cocked his head to the left. "It's not?"

I took my husband by the hand and led him outside. I saw the two of us, Emilola and Kareem, six, playing there under my orange tree.

"Kareem had this perfectly round face," I began. "And big eyes, and these sweeping eyelashes. He cradled his head with his palms when I showed him my loose tooth. After I pulled it out, he puked all over my leg. I ordered him to wipe it with his shirt. He begged me to let him leave. I told him we were born on the same day, we used the same first words, all the same stuff we always said to each other. So, of course we should lose our first tooth on the same day, right? So stupid. He started screaming even before that rock was in my hand."

Matthew tensed his breath.

"Kareem's hands went over his mouth. I ordered him to remove them, and his scream still sits inside my fucking skin."

Matthew exhaled. "Jesus!"

"I know! I was a total asshole kid. He even has this really hideous scar."

"Well, you definitely need to go see him."

I nodded. "I do."

"Listen, I get it. But I also only see that sparkle in your eyes when you say his name."

"Matt, it's not like that—"

"Shh," he said, and he took my hand. "You have a beautiful smile, Ems. I don't want to be the reason it dies again. Go."

DADDY PAID TO HELP me get my license. A week later, I was helping Fatima into the front seat of my father's car. We moved, surrounded by quiet for the first half of the drive. Her tight grin suddenly spread into a luminous smile.

"You are happy?" I asked.

She nodded.

"Do you have a picture of Kareem?"

"Ah! No. I want to enjoy the look on Kareem's face when he sees you, and yours when you see him." I could feel her smiling at me.

"Does he know I am coming?"

Fatima turned to the window, muttering.

I glared over at her. We were almost there. "I cannot just show up for his wedding."

"Why not?" she probed, casting a stern expression my way.

"Because," I replied in English. "Just because."

"Why not?" she repeated, with a hand funneled over her ear. "Were you not born on the same day?"

My stomach roiled. "Don't say that."

"Did you not walk and talk at the same time?"

"Please, stop."

Her hands danced as if speaking a language of their own. "*Walai*, did you not live like brother and sister? Who will stop you if you walk in with me, Emilola? Even when I am dead, this thing that ties us can never be broken. I know I am not your mother, God rest her soul, but you, He decided long before any of us came here, are my daughter. Full stop." She let her eyes wander out the window.

"You cannot do things that way. I'm afraid—what if his fiancé does not want extra guests?"

Fatima clapped her hands, loudly, and the noise resounded inside my skull. "How are you a guest? Let that stupid girl open her mouth, I will show her one plus one."

Shaking my head, I chuckled at her awakened feistiness.

"I hope I never vex you," I said.

She rested a hand on my knee. "God forbid, dear. You are an angel. Moody, but kind."

"I am not kind."

"You are. Who would know more than me?"

I glanced over at her. "Kareem."

Her hand left my knee to sit in her lap.

I began, "That scar on Kareem's mouth?"

Fatima nodded. "Yes, he told me what happened."

"What did he tell you?"

"That Chimaka beat him."

"That's what he said?"

"Yes, now. Just before you left for America, Kareem confessed to me. He said Chimaka was always beating him. I told your Daddy and he sacked Chimaka's father that evening. But then Kareem cried and cried as if he had lost his right arm."

Water gathered in the pits of my arms. I said, "I am a worse person than I thought."

"Why, my dear?"

"Kareem deserved better."

Fatima waved her hand. "You carry too much load for your head."

I nodded. "That may be true, but damn it. Poor Kareem. I—I have to tell you something."

She held up her hand. After a stretched breath, she said, "Love is stranger than a dog wearing trousers. You know, I loved Kareem's father very much—I thought so, at least. But he did not want a family, so I did not tell him Kareem was his son."

"My God! Really?"

"I got him a job driving for your father—to keep him close. Maybe one day he would change after watching Kareem grow."

"Daddy's old driver was Kareem's father?"

"Yes, yes. I prayed for him to do right with the opportunity—driving for a banker is not a small thing, now."

"What ever happened to him?"

"I don't know."

"Kareem told me that Daddy beat him for stealing from him."

"No one stole me." She winked.

"You?"

"Listen, if a worm sticks its head out of the ground at the wrong time, it can't be surprised if a bird snatches it, now."

"What does that mean?"

"Kareem's father chose me too late."

"Wait? You and Daddy?"

She shrugged. "Do not trouble yourself, *sha*."

"I should have known."

Her emphatic sigh penetrated the air. "I was so angry with you that day, I could not stop crying. On the way to the hospital, *ehn*, I almost reached back to knock your head. Your daddy stopped my hand and begged me with his eyes. Then, I saw that he had been crying too. He loved my son the way I loved my son, and soon, one plus one became two."

"You both knew?"

"*Ah ahn?*"

"Why didn't you say?"

"Who knows. And when Kareem told me it was Chimaka, I was sad to let him lose a friend, but he needed to learn that sacrifices come with consequences."

"Auntie Fatima, I spent years worried Kareem would tell."

She shrugged. "You and Kareem are not the only ones with secrets. You are both like me—you cut away the bad to keep the good. Listen, you left as a troubled child and returned as a lovely woman. But one thing is missing, I can tell."

"What?"

"When you first came back, I asked how you were, you remember?"

I nodded.

"You listed things: I am a lawyer, my son this, my son that, my house, my car, you even pushed that Professor Matthew up front like a freshly roasted goat for everyone to salivate over. I did not once hear you say, 'I am happy.'"

"Aren't you the one who says, 'The dancing rooster does not yet know its fate'?"

Her hand topped my knee again. "Emilola, you are not a rooster. You are a hen."

Together, we laughed until the silence returned.

Once we settled in the hotel room, Fatima called Kareem on the telephone. They spoke Hausa. I had a feeling she did not mention me. I heard his garbled voice floating from the speaker, but his face remained a hodgepodge of every man I had ever seen.

"He is coming," she said. "You will be my surprise."

After resting, showering, and dressing, I needed a drink to settle my nerves. I called out to Fatima as she dressed in the bathroom, "I'm going downstairs."

The elevator opened. I stepped inside. The etchings in the mirror splattered my image in a million pieces. There I was, overly made up, with loosely-curled hair, and my body squeezed into every inch of a cocktail dress.

"What the fuck are you doing?" I muttered, smearing my lipstick into my palm.

I watched the numbers as the elevator went down until the doors opened for me.

Three people waited to enter. I exited, and headed for the bar. Two shots of Jameson whiskey came, and I took them quickly before requesting the check. "I am in room 9-1-5." The warmth in my chest began to relax me. I was ready to face anything and anyone. At the elevator, I kept my head low. A woman rushed out with a hand on her brow, as if the ride exhausted her.

An apology came from the man in there. I gave him a wave of my hand on the way in. "It's cool," I said. "Must be man problems."

"What makes you say that?" he asked.

"Because I know that look on her face."

"Is that right?"

"Totally. A man pissed that woman off. Ninth floor, please."

A steady roar lifted us. We rocked from side to side in fixed silence. He turned to me and said, "I am her man."

"Excuse me?"

"The woman just now—I am her man. And I did not upset her."

I held up my hands. "Whoa. I didn't mean anything by it. I was just projecting my own issues."

He grunted.

"Listen, this went way left." I offered my hand. "Start over?"

He nodded and extended his hand as well. "Sure. My name is Kareem," he said.

My knees rattled while I searched for my words. "My name is Emilola, Kareem. I drove your mother here."

"Emi? Lola?" His eyes widened. "Emilola?"

He patted my head and shoulders as if confirming I was real. Had there been sand around, he would have tossed a handful at me to ensure I was not a ghost. I nodded as he excitedly shook my hand. Looking up at him, I saw the same boy from my past with that crooked scar I carved into his face. The mark now enlivened his smile, resting above gleaming white teeth, as two dimples sank into his cheeks. He stood in confidence, too sturdy to have evolved from the ungainly boy I once knew. His thick arms went around me, and I wished that I could meld into him as perfectly as that scar. I smiled when he freed me and caught myself staring into his inky black eyes. "It has been a few years," I said.

He replied, "A lifetime."

The doors opened. I hoped they would shut again, and we would be returned to 1986, when Emilola and Kareem, eleven, were sitting under my orange tree talking about who we would marry. I had described a tall, strong, handsome Yoruba man, and Kareem had said, "You. I want to marry you, Emi." I stroked his scar that day and felt drawn to him in a strange way. Before I could tell him, Chimaka started shouting about a sword.

Standing before Kareem again, after dreaming of the moment for years, I felt the same pull toward him. I leaned in. He did too. I dropped my gaze and stepped back.

Once outside the elevator, I walked briskly. "Your mother is in room 915," I said.

Trailing behind, Kareem intoned, "Wait. Emilola."

I marched ahead, hoping he had focused only on my face and not my overburdened dress or wispy hair.

"Slow down!" he ordered.

I paused.

When Kareem finally reached me, he caught and released his breath. His hands rested on my shoulders. "Emi, please. Let me just look at you for a moment."

My fingers caressed the rough skin that filled the fissure across his lip. "I'm so sorry," I cried.

He smiled. "It's in the past."

"Kareem, why so forgiving?"

He shrugged.

I said, "Please, don't do that."

"Emi, do you know why I said the day this happened was the best day of my life?"

"Because you rode in Daddy's car?"

He held both my hands. "No. Because my first ride in his car was with you."

Fatima opened the door and called out to him. "Kareem, you see who I brought?"

He walked toward his mother, stopped and prostrated before her. "Mama, afternoon, mah." When he rose, they embraced outside the room, I ran inside to hide my tears.

"Emilola, we are going," I heard Fatima say through the crack in the door. "Will you come down?"

"Yes. I'll meet you downstairs."

The door shut behind them. Purse in hand, I stepped out of the room and strolled down the hall. I composed myself with deep breaths until I reached the elevator. When the doors opened, Kareem was in it, alone.

"Where's your mother?" I asked, peering about as if he was hiding her.

"She is downstairs."

I attempted to step around him, but he hooked me with that languid expression. Water pooled at the rims of his eyes. Water spilled from mine. We stayed connected in the silence between us until Kareem's hands went over his heart. He planted his foot between the closing doors, pulled me inside, and we rode the elevator down, hand in hand.

THIEF

LYNN HAD BEEN SIXTEEN for only two weeks. The clouds shifted, giving a glimpse of the sun as she strolled by. Beneath her brilliant red mane was an equally bold smile. Eyes from men and women quietly buzzing over their meals followed as she confidently stepped into the café to stand in line. She had no inkling of the power she held when she entered a room.

The man behind her cleared his throat. It was as if he had been placed there to pluck her from this childish obscurity. She turned around. He was easily a decade older. She could not have known that the way his teeth shone like a full moon was how he snared his victims. Not much else was required on his part once she caught a glimpse of his smile; and after that fate-sealing wink, he continued with a simple, "Hello."

She nodded.

"Do you often carry the sun with you?" he asked, in a thick French accent.

She nearly allowed her rose-tinted pout to curl into a smile before her brain calculated that this had been a weak line. She delivered a disappointed frown.

"Okay, that wasn't a great line," he said. "But when a woman as beautiful as you falls into my world, my nerves are rattled. Can you blame me?"

The ecru white of her cheeks flushed and her flawless hand hid an unexpected chuckle. She was unversed at being wooed or being called a woman for that matter—so she took the compliment and returned a sweet, simple smile.

"You can thank me by at least telling me your name," he added, still grinning.

She saw in his eyes a bit of hope toward carrying the moment into more than a chance meeting. She raised her iPhone for a glimpse at the time, then decided to help the flirting along.

"Lynn. My name is Lynn, and thank you."

"I'm Pierre. What will you take?" he pulled apart his wallet. "It's on me."

"A hot chocolate, please; extra hot," she said, mouthing the words in a slight whimper.

He requested one espresso and a *petit four*. "Plus one hot chocolate, extra hot," he added, mocking her girlish disposition. She laughed.

They should take their drinks at an open table outside, he suggested, and she followed. He preferred to eat in open spaces—for the privilege, he said, speaking as if they were long-lost friends.

Outside, he pulled out her chair. "Sit," he pressed. "Unless you have somewhere else to be."

"No. I'm here on vacation from the States with my parents. They're probably sick of me. I'm supposed to go have a long lunch."

After taking his seat as well, he pointed toward the Eiffel Tower.

"What?" she asked, searching the sky.

He replied, "The sun's face hanging behind the tower like that? I'm going to paint it, differently, like nobody has ever done."

With wide eyes, she asked, "You're a painter?"

"No. *Un Artiste*? *Oui*. And not just painting—I tell stories on canvas, and I dabble in writing too." He pointed again. "What do you see there?"

"The tower?"

He dropped his face in disappointment within his palms. "No. Me? I see a tall, slender woman. The sun lingers behind her like a dutiful lover. Her lover rarely shows his face, but today, he comes to kiss the back of her neck ever so gently."

Slow to catch the interpretation, Lynn smiled. "Oh—I see what you're sayin'."

Lynn's American accent did little to hide her youthful witlessness. She asked his age and immediately felt foolish. "Sorry, I shouldn't ask you that."

"No bother. I'm twenty-seven. You?"

She chuckled nervously, "I'm a lot younger than that."

He shrugged. "Just a number." Leaning into her cheeky effervescence, he added, "It doesn't matter."

She cooed as he described himself as a lost soul finding his way through the world. Taking measured sips of her hot chocolate seemed the more mature way. When she spoke, she saw him taunted by her East Coast lisp.

"This is my first time here in Paris, but I've basically seen all of Europe," she said.

"Oh—well, you should go to Africa one day. I say that every human being should experience it at least once. It simply changes your soul."

"My mother would disagree. My father is Nigerian, but I've never been there. He goes back to Africa without us—not sure why. Mom is American and we live in Manhattan."

"I traveled through West Africa after I left University. It was the happiest three years of my life—too much chocolate for one man."

Lynn rolled her eyes, miffed by the comparison between race and confection. "I should tell you," she began, before her attention was lost to the hovering clouds above. As the first few drops fell, they threatened to ruin her neatly placed curls.

"Why I did anything to my hair today, I'll never know."

Instinctively, he presented his fedora. "Unless you want my jacket?"

"No, I like this hat," she sang, setting it firmly on her head.

The rain looked to be getting heavier, and other customers dispersed from their tables. Pierre said, "Let's go back inside."

"No. Let's go someplace else," she answered, with a suggestive wink and a nod. One of her hands held his hat still, while the other sat atop his hand, implicitly flirting.

Something behind her scandalous eyes lured him in. He was not surprised by her quick acceptance, yet he raised an eyebrow and the side of his mouth. "I know just the place."

The word *okay* fell off her lips as easily as it formed in her head.

Trapped inside Pierre's embrace as they walked, she squeezed him tight. They stopped at the Gallerie Devoux, just a block from the cafe. The glass wall separated them from a display of neatly placed canvases splattered with oil and ink. Lynn squeezed tighter as he pointed out his favorites. A faction of cheerful women waved at Pierre from inside the gallery, catching Lynn's attention more than his.

"Let's go," Lynn said, securing Pierre by the elbow. He faced her with his own glowing grin. She blinked off rain.

They galloped over puddles and her dainty steps blended with his cumbersome ones, drumming up a chorus to their destination. Precisely nine flats were nestled within that building, and she tilted her head to capture its megalithic stature.

"This is what I love most about Paris," she sang. "A romantic touch built this place from the ground on up; don't ya think?"

"I pegged you right, then," he said, fiddling with his keys in the rain-soaked egress. "An American smitten by French romance, no?"

She sighed, enamored by ardor while tracing the length of his torso to the tip of his chin with her eyes. Right there, he lifted her like the *petit four* he had recently devoured and placed a kiss on the rouge of her cheeks.

"One for each lifetime I would have to return to find a match to your beauty," he whispered, leaving his breath against her neck.

Yes, yes, yes, poured from the millions of pores on her body, as if he touched each and every one. She was begging, heaving through the stillness of the moment, as if capable of bursting through her own skin.

"My flat is on the fifth floor," Pierre said, and again, she followed.

The door opened up to a shadowy room. The walls inside were covered with pictures of near-nude women and mud-cloth tapestry. Newspapers and magazines were strewn about and the queen-size bed sat in the center of the room. Easels stood like watchmen with unfinished faces overlooking the bed. Lingering in the chilly air was the perfume of cigarettes and incense disintegrated into ashes. An open tin can of snuff was on the bedside table. Unsure of what it was, she avoided staring at it for too long even as her eyes went back to it again and again. The rush of an impending encounter quickly fizzled when Pierre slammed the door behind them. The sound threw her off kilter. Lynn felt her heart begin to race within her body. When a cast-iron latch sealed them in, Lynn felt her palms dampen and she buried them inside the pockets of her sweater.

"You are not nervous, are you?" he asked, watching her once-daring arms now cradle her center.

"No," she said, hiding behind a brewing innocence.

Slipped out of the fantasy, she watched Pierre take a seat on the bed. He pinched the snuff and lifted it to his nostrils, inhaling deeply. After wiping the excess powder off the tip of his nose, he pointed a remote control at the stereo. "Music?"

"Sure." She chuckled.

He patted a spot next to him. "Sit down," he pleaded.

She joined him. He placed a hand on her thigh. She tightened beneath his grip. He unbuttoned her sweater and gently rolled down the sleeves. He placed one arm around her lower back while tilting her top half with the other. She took a deep breath.

He kissed her, but not as she had imagined. Her lips were pried apart and his tongue darted for her throat. She moved her head to gain some balance, but he held her still, suckling her tongue like a famished calf.

"Wait. I can't—" she said.

"Stop talking."

"Wait," she cried.

But waiting was not for him.

"Don't or I'll scream."

His hand smeared the gloss from her lips, signaling movement into the next phase of their chance meeting. She thrashed about. Her flailing arms and legs worked tirelessly when her mouth could not, and his weight kept her still. He dragged his tongue delicately across her face. The breath that carried his whispers was foul and dingy like his room, and she felt queasy at the thought of experiencing him. He gorged himself on her fight, growing swiftly from it.

Having been warned of the pain that comes with being touched by a man and feeling sunk by the voluminous music in the air, Lynn tearfully awaited it. She thought of her mother, and what her eyes would display when she found out. As if Pierre could sense Lynn's mind wandering, he pinched her skin with his teeth and bite marks ran from her chest on down. His hand started a gentle massage on her navel. She closed her eyes, shaking her head *no* and wishing for a way out of there—but his fingers were inside her, pushing and pulling for something she had always been told to keep to private.

Lynn braced herself. Pierre pushed his way in, breaking her trust in men forever. Her tightness fell away with every thrust until she was wholly defeated.

There she lied, melting in a pool of guilt and sadness and relief while Pierre breathed a satisfied sigh. He slipped open the drawer next to the bed and reached inside. He removed two things. One was a cigarette and the other was a towel.

"What's going to happen when I unlock that door?" he asked, after handing her the cloth.

Tears slipped from the corners of her eyes. "Nothing," she whimpered. "I just want to go home."

He dragged his silhouette near the window and looked straight ahead. He said, "I am not a monster, you know," reverting to his formerly gentle self.

Lynn gathered her clothes and rushed down five flights of stairs without looking back.

NO MORE TROUBLE

Jonnie did not stop running until he collided with the thunderous echo of voices at the market. After catching his breath, he found no one chasing him. Shirtless and barefoot, he walked aimlessly, pulled by the merged aromas of wood-roasted meat, peppery stew, and frying fish. His stomach answered the call with a grumble. While he was doubled over, trying to calm the grievance within, he noticed a girl sitting on a stool.

He tried to sever his gaze, only to find his eyes returned to where she sat. Her pockmarked face held a wide smile. Her eyes carried light. Her fingers danced sensually with every stroke of a knife around the oranges she sliced to order. Penned by a bevy of customers, she had not noticed him staring at her until he pushed his way through to the front. She glanced up at him to cue his order. He kept a grin as if rendered mute. She spoke mellifluously, "How many orange you want?"

His own words were lodged inside his throat.

Sharply, she asked, "*Wetin* you want, now?"

He raised an index finger.

Spinning the orange in one hand while the other ran a blade

around the skin of the fruit, she kept her eyes on him. Jonnie nodded through the silence. He did not know what to call the jumbled feelings coursing through him. His heart was still beating from his eventful morning. The rest of him persisted under shock by the small-framed beauty sitting before him. When the orange peel fell in one continuous coil, it pulled Jonnie's attention to the ground. The girl snapped her fingers at him. "You want make I cut am?"

He snapped out of his trance, then blinked wildly as if something in his head had broken. Once able to speak, he shrugged. "No cut am, *abeg*."

"Take."

"How much?" he asked.

"Fifty naira," she told him, eyeing the pockets of his tattered trousers.

He handed over a one-hundred-naira note. "I *dash* you change," he said, nodding with confidence.

She offered him two more unpeeled oranges. The boy refused. "Then take four." She was almost begging. He needed the food, she could tell by the way the skin on his torso rippled over his ribs.

"No, no, no," he said. "One plenty."

The odd lowness about his way made her think he was a *mumu* like the young men who smoked *igbo* and roamed the market laughing at imagined worlds. He probably also stole food to survive and picked pockets. But she saw life hanging behind his eyes, and placidity in the way he moved through the chaos surrounding them. It hooked her from the moment he had accepted the orange without allowing his eyes to leave hers. So, she peeled another orange, sliced it in half and gave it to him.

"My name *nah* Margaret."

"I be Jonathan." He slapped his chest. "*Dem dey* call me Jonnie."

"Okay, Jonnie. *Chop*."

He bit into the orange quickly, licking juice off his fingers as he chewed the whole thing, through to the bitterness of the seeds. Margaret gave him another. Before he could refuse, she yelled, "Eat—now!"

As his body settled, seemingly relieved from inside out, he said, "*Tank* you."

She nodded.

He went around her, quietly collecting orange peels. She shook her head, believing he planned to eat the rinds he gathered.

"*Abeg*, make I borrow one bag?" he pleaded, eyeing the cluster of nylon sacks at her feet.

"No problem. Take."

The wave of customers at lunchtime swept in and out. By evening, Jonnie had gathered seven full bags of rinds. She asked what he planned to do with them.

"For kill mosquito."

She smiled; relieved it was not to be his next meal.

After Margaret sold her last orange, she upturned the bin. "I *don* finish work."

"Where you *dey* go, now?" he asked.

"I *dey* go buy more orange make I sell tomorrow. Then I *go go* for my house."

The enthusiasm drained from his eyes. "*Shay* you go come here again?"

She nodded. "Where you *dey* go?"

"*Wit* you," he answered, smiling. "I fit come *wit* you?"

She took his hand. "Come."

Following behind a crowd, they walked side by side. Jonnie carried her bin. His words, beginning with a stutter, suddenly flowed like an endless tap of intricate tales, drawing Margaret out of her skin and dropping her in his world. Margaret stayed there, concerned about a boy sold by his distraught father after his mother's death. Jonnie showed her the jagged scar on his left shoulder. It had become part of him when he jumped off the moving truck as it stole into the night with unwanted children. When her fingers traced the warped lines sewn into his skin, he remained steady. It was the first human caress he had had in as long as he could remember.

Jonnie said to Margaret when her hand left his body, "No

worry, Margaret. When bad *ting* happen, God even come bless me, every time."

She shrugged.

Margaret noticed the setting sun had dipped out of view. Across the sky, the windswept shades of grey signaled the beginning of an ending she did not yet want. She took his hand and led their strides. Outside the back entrance to Mr. Singh's pharmacy, they stood alone. Waiting for the door to open, they stared at each other. Jonnie felt locked in a place where earth and sky had come to meet. Her face was perfect. She saw an innocuous boy whose body reeked of fear as if constantly expecting danger. Their fingers intertwined. She giggled and brought a hand over her mouth to conceal her teeth.

"You fine," he told her, peeling the mask off her smile.

"Wait here," she said. "I *dey* come."

He did not know what to do with the strange feeling roused by her, but he hoped with clasped hands that she was not another fleeting person in his life.

When Margaret returned with a box of oranges, a full sack of groundnuts, some okra, and a whole roasted chicken encased in plastic, Jonnie gasped. "*Ehn!* From where you collect all *dis* one?"

"I sell orange, bring Mr. Singh him money. Tomorrow, I come back, same *ting*. Mr. Singh, *nah* good man from India. Him *dash* me *dis* chicken and groundnut *sef*. Make we *dey* go?"

Jonnie's eyes widened. "Yes."

Margaret lived in a structure of cement and wood. Mold coated the walls of the corridor that parted five rooms to each side of the building.

"I get small room," she told him.

It sat at the end of the malodorous hallway. They walked through the auburn glow of three kerosene lanterns hanging from the ceiling. The window in Margaret's room overlooked a decrepit well out back. She lit a candle and carried its dancing flame to the table beside her mat. Jonnie sat on the floor near the door. Margaret said she rented from Mr. Singh, and paid less than others in the building because she sold things for him.

Jonnie licked his index finger and pointed to the sky. "*Dis* Mr. Singh, *nah* blessing from God-*o*."

She nodded. "*Nah* so."

Jonnie asked her age. She stiffened her neck and said, "Twenty." He was nineteen, spent over half his life sleeping outdoors, and had woken up in a stranger's car just that morning. She told him she had fended for herself for as long as she had known she was alive. But her story had been less eventful than his. One day she had parents; the next, she did not.

She shrugged. "But I no vex. *Nah* so life *dey*, *sha*."

"Life hard, *sha*," he said. "Life plenty simple for woman, no be so?"

"Woman suffer like man-*o*. But woman get *bettah* sense."

Life had shown him that privileged people required their egos stroked by the less fortunate, so he chuckled, an ddecided to agree with whatever Margaret said.

While waiting for the chicken to simmer in an oily stew of tomatoes, okra, and peppers, they played Ludo. Before Jonnie tossed the dice across the board, he held them in his palms, covered them with his breath and shouted, "*Numbah sis*," as they tumbled. He asked Margaret to move his peg for him. She counted to five. The next time, he shouted, "*Tiri*," and again she moved his peg. When he shouted, "Sisteen," before the throw, she chuckled. He froze, knowing he had let it show just how little he knew about counting. She placed a hand on his. Seeing her smile, his shoulders sank with relief. They laughed to each other's stories, until all of Margaret's pegs reached home. She danced to celebrate her win.

Later, Jonnie rounded *garri* neatly between his thumb and fingers to sop up the viscous stew. He hurriedly shoved food into his mouth, dripping sauce down his chin. He did not wait to swallow before gathering more, and he chewed chicken meat hastily and crushed the bones into splinters, licking each one of his fingers as he went. Margaret offered more when his bowl was clear. He did not stop thanking her, even after she washed their dishes and they both sat on the threadbare mat listening to music streaming in through the window. She placed a finger to his lips. "No problem."

Staring at the candle's fading light, he asked himself, *Shay make I dey go abi make I stay?* As if hearing the words inside his head, Margaret beckoned him to stand. She rose off the mat too. Her head pressed against his bony chest and she inhaled the musty perfume of his sweat. She pulled him so close that if they fused into one, it would not have surprised her. He grew firm when he felt her tongue on his. She panted through his thrusts, and after, they lay gazing at the gossamer cobwebs cast across the ceiling. Neither spoke. Margaret broke the chorus of their heavy breaths with a cough.

She faced him. "*Shay* you love me?"

Jonnie awaited love's deafening entrance from a bolt of lightning or God's whispers or string music, as he had seen on television. Feeling not quite riveted by the silence, he looked on in aimless thought. Margaret nudged him, tight-lipped and engrossed by the trilling in her stomach. For the first time, he noticed the thuds in his chest detached from fear—could it be love? Forfeiting want for need, he pressed his lips to hers.

"Yes."

She smiled.

IN THE MORNING, JONNIE had pulled well water and boiled it for tea before Margaret awakened. He helped her carry oranges to the market and collected more peels for drying while she worked. She expressed her own affections with food, and over a few weeks, had packed more meat onto his bones and restored life inside his eyes. They carried on this way for two months until Mr. Singh found Jonnie sleeping in the room when he performed an impromptu check on the building. Jonnie assured Margaret, "I go find work," when she told him Mr. Singh was raising her rent if he stayed.

By day, Jonnie waited outside the gate of a private school in Ikoyi. Dressed in ragged knickers, a sweater vest with more holes than knit and a pair of clear rubber sandals, he smiled and waved his sign each time a car swept past. By evening, he crawled back to Margaret, empty-handed again.

"Tomorrow, grace of God," he promised.

She stared at his hands and spoke with unaffected stoicism. "Tell me, *shay nah* grace of God go put food inside your *bele*?"

Next morning, Jonnie returned to the school, looking haggard from the argument-filled night. He tucked himself behind a primped bush, and waited. Straight-faced, and moved by sheer resolve, he approached the grandiose gates of the school's compound. He prostrated before the stocky security guards to greet them. "Good morning—" The words did not fall off his lips before he felt their batons across his back and took off running.

Running, running, and again running. The last time he ran with such purpose, just before he saw Margaret for the first time, he had just been dragged out of a stranger's car for sleeping in it. Before that, he narrowly escaped the rubber tire tossed around him for stealing at the market. Before that, he had followed a man into an alley, allowed his hand to enter the man's trousers, and accepted money. After, he ran, ashamed, running as speedily as he ran from these guards. Devotion to God in that moment turned to anger, and anger forced him still. "God," he shouted. "Help me!"

The following week, Jonnie reappeared, better dressed in a collared white shirt and tie-up *ankara* trousers, asking to meet with the owner of the school. The guards chuckled until he shrank inside their unruly laughter. The week after that, he returned dressed the same, chugging down the affluent quietude of Corona Estates Avenue. Amid the chirping of birds leaping from tree to tree, Jonnie dragged himself along the paved road, flanked by stark white stucco fences. Although the sign around his neck assured that he was *Trustworthy* and *God-fearing,* he wanted it to read, *Two days, I no chop food.*

MARGARET WAS IN THE backyard hand-washing clothes. Her neighbor—Chinyere, a thick-armed woman—tugged on a rope to draw water from the well. She emptied the pail into a basin and carried it near Margaret. After retightening the wrapper around the sleeping baby on her back, Chinyere bent to scrub an empty soup pot.

"How now, Margaret?" she asked.

Margaret looked up. "Small by small, I *dey* try, *sha.*"

"*Shay* Jonnie find work?"

Margaret knew Chinyere pursued fodder for gossip. Even so, she replied, "Morning to night, he *dey* try." She hoped Chinyere would spread stories of Jonnie's diligence instead.

Chinyere nodded, sucking her teeth. "Soon, now. Grace of God."

Margaret rolled her eyes. "Yes, God and grace."

Chinyere pointed to the sky.

Wiping her nose, Margaret sighed. "Everything *dey* smell, *sha.* Even orange scent *dey* trouble me." In an attempt to rise off her knees, she staggered backward.

"Careful, now," Chinyere sang.

Margaret fanned herself with her hand.

Chinyere lifted a cup to Margaret's lips. "Sit, sit. You *chop* food today?"

"No be food *wahala, o,*" Margaret said, rubbing her abdomen.

Chinyere's jaws fell. "*Ah, dat nah* different trouble. You get *bele*? How many month?"

Margaret shrugged her shoulders. "I no know. One, two *sef.*"

"Why you no tell me? *Shay* Jonnie know?"

A bit miffed, Margaret groaned. "*Sebi nah* him be the *fada.*

Yes, Jonnie know." That was not true, but she planned to tell him soon. He would be ecstatic, she was sure. He loved her. He had told her so.

Later, Margaret rested on the mat in her room, awaiting Jonnie's arrival. When he came in, he planted himself beside her. Unwilling to start the night's inevitable argument, he remained silent. She sat. He got up and peeled off his shirt and trousers. Standing before the window, he stared achingly at nothing in particular. Margaret joined him there with her arms around his middle. "Jonnie, *wetin* happen?"

He avoided turning around, speaking now as if rapt in dialogue with the well outside. He mentioned the spasms in his stomach, his broken spirit, feeling lost in God's silence. Margaret stepped between him and the window and pressed her finger to his lips. "Shh. *Fest, chop* small, small," she said. "Chinyere *dash* us rice and stew."

He sat on the mat. His mouth took quick handfuls of the food until he licked the bowl and his fingers clean. Usually, with food in his stomach and his body settled, his eyes glistened to signal interest in her. Even with her kiss, he remained rigid to her touch.

"Why?" she asked.

His face betrayed nothing.

She stretched her plea, "Why, Jonnie?"

"Because—"

Margaret wrapped her legs around him, nudged him with a hand on his chin and whined, "Why, now?"

He answered, "Because I no want make you get *bele*."

She scooted away from him. Her knees to her chest, she rocked. She wished she had told him sooner, or showed signs: the vomiting, the exhaustion, the heightened sense of smell, the uncontrollable mood swings. Jonnie saw her eyes darting back and forth and he moved near.

"Margaret, no vex. I no fit find work. If we born *pikin*, life go hard pass *dis*."

Margaret rose. He stood too. With crossed fingers atop her head, she let his words embed themselves deep inside her soul, where she needed to hear them—for they could not be truly consumed by her ears alone.

He repeated, "No *pikin*! We no get money for rent, no food, how baby go *chop*?"

She shoved him in the chest. He fell. She pinned him there with her glare. He saw her chest rising and falling rapidly.

"*Wetin*, now?" he asked.

Her breathing was spaced now—deep breaths intermittent with speedy ones—as if the room grew stingy with its air. She turned her back to him. They now stood on opposite sides of the room.

Margaret pointed to the door. "*Commot* from here, now, now!"

Jonnie's hands cradled his skull. "Why?"

"Out!" She had never raised her voice with so much freedom.

From behind, he caressed her shoulders, spoke softly. "Why?"

"Because," she said, defeated. "I *don* get *bele*."

He spun her around, squeezed the meat of her arms. Her eyes swelled with tears and she trembled within his hold. Jonnie wished he had released her sooner. He wished her eyes were not so red and staring painfully at his. He wished he had yielded to her touch. He wished he was lying on the mat beside her, inside her, loving her instead.

"Useless *ting*," she spat. "No come back here, again, *o*. I go do *abuhshun*. Get out!"

What he wouldn't do to take back the rise of his hand, its sound across her cheek, her scream. Instead, he belted out the room.

CHINYERE RATTLED HER KNUCKLES against Margaret's door after Jonnie sped past her. She whispered, "Margaret, *nah* Chinyere."

Inside, Margaret sat with propped knees. Her body looked

small pressed into the corner bathed in the candle's light. She looked up. Chinyere knelt beside her.

"*Wetin* happen?" Chinyere begged.

Margaret swept up her skirt against unrelenting tears. When her words firmed enough to leave her mouth, she said, "Jonnie say no *pikin*."

"*Osi gini*. Why?"

Margaret shrugged. His reasons were irrelevant.

Chinyere put her arms around her, stretching her words, "Margaret, tell me now. Why?"

"Him say because him no fit find work."

Chinyere rose off the floor, aghast by the news. "*Ah*, Jesus Christ! This boy no get sense-*o*. *Sebi* you say him know already?"

"Him no know," Margaret said. Her head hung low. "I just tell am today."

No need to beat the dead. "Woman *dey* suffer plenty for *dis* world-*o*," Chinyere said.

"*Wetin* I go do now?" Margaret wailed, wishing she had told Jonnie sooner, wishing that none of it ever happened.

Chinyere kept Margaret in a tight embrace and whispered, "Real question: *wetin* you *wan* do?"

Margaret would not reveal the worst place her thoughts had led her to—the thing she had said to Jonnie that caused him to slap her as if meaning to shake the idea out of her head.

Chinyere whispered, "*Abuhshun*."

"No," Margaret scowled.

Chinyere rested a hand on Margaret's knee. "You see me? I get six *pikin*, small room, husband *wey* drink like fish. I *don* suffer, *o*. But woman no supposed to *dey* suffer, suffer for world, you hear?"

Margaret sighed. "How *dem* go do *abuhshun*?"

Chinyere shook her head. "You take two tablet, sit for toilet, no more *wahala*."

Margaret shook her head vigorously. "Jonnie no go 'gree."

Chinyere lifted Margaret's chin so their eyes met. "Johnnie no go know." They sat in a swirl of silence until Chinyere said, "We *go go* Mr. Singh pharmacy."

"When?" Margaret asked, too exhausted to argue.

"Tomorrow."

JONNIE AWAKENED TO A cock's crow. He rubbed his eyes, yawned, and felt the soft crumble of red earth beneath him. The sky pulled back its skin. Jonnie looked up. A smile flowering from his thoughts of becoming a father brightened his face. Head high, he decided to begin another day's quest for work.

On the other side of town, Margaret and Chinyere waited outside the pharmacy for Mr. Singh. After letting them in, Mr. Singh barked orders at his assistant from behind the counter. Margaret stared at the Indian man's head of slick black hair and the nest of salt and pepper fuzz peering through the unbuttoned top of his shirt. Sweat slid from his forehead. "Five minutes," he mouthed.

Margaret thought Jonnie would probably join her in whispering about Mr. Singh's unruly chest hair and saturated face. Jonnie would have said the man looked like he ate a whole plate of plantains and smeared grease all over himself. She would have agreed, and maybe they would have fallen over each other in amusement. She laughed aloud at the thought.

Chinyere asked, "Margaret, *wetin dey* do you, now? Why you *dey* laughing?"

Margaret looked down. "Nothing."

Mr. Singh called them in.

JONNIE WAS RESTING IN the shade of an almond tree, tugging on God's ears with his pleas, when the tinted window of a glossy black sedan rolled down. A woman's voice floated out, "Young man?"

He lifted his head. "Yes, mah?"

"Come."

He darted toward the vehicle.

"Afternoon, mah."

"I've seen you by my daughter's school before. Are you looking for work?"

Jonnie nodded. "Ah, *anyting* mah. Clean house. Cook. I cut garden. *Cahpentah*, everyting."

"Good. I need a gardener."

"Yes, mah. I cut garden."

"Okay, enter the front."

The woman's driver unlocked the doors. Jonnie climbed in excitedly, nodding to the occupants as he entered. He placed his sign beneath his feet. The car began to move. The windows trundled up, controlled by the driver's push of a button. A breeze whirred through the small slats in the dashboard. Jonnie inhaled the brisk air, using his forearm to soak up the sweat on his brow. He turned around. The butter-skinned woman briefly raised her head from her telephone to smile at him. He smiled back. Beside the woman, a round-faced girl of no more than sixteen quietly stared out of the window, slurping a bubbly orange drink.

No one asked for Jonnie's name, yet he offered it behind hurried breaths. "My name *nah* Jonathan, mah, but people *dem* call me Jonnie."

There was no response to this announcement. Margaret would have known not to do that, not to forget her place. He restored himself in silence, staring ahead.

When the girl belched, the cabin filled with a faint citrus smell. It reminded him of Margaret. He imagined sharing the news about his work. Her delight, he hoped, would bring back her smile. He would rub her growing abdomen and feet, bring her Choco-Milo cubes, and cuddle beside her and their newborn son. He would tell her of the moment that love finally struck him—right there, in the strange woman's vehicle, when he pictured Margaret heavy with their baby.

As the car turned onto Badger Avenue, Jonnie looked up and around. They were immersed in the tranquility of those who could afford to live behind walls. The fences sat high—some made of steel; others, stucco; all with broken bottles bonded along the tops. Jonnie watched with bridled awe as two cast-iron gates slithered apart to expose a water fountain. He stared up at the brick façade of the house and gasped.

The driver parked, and Jonnie climbed out after him.

After helping the woman out of the car, the driver escorted her up the concrete pavement. The girl came out next, lugging a heavy bookbag. Jonnie raced around to her side, and extended his hand to help her up the steps. She slapped his hand away and walked past him to cautiously follow the railing up. Jonnie's eyes tailed the girl's bouncy walk up opulent stairs that led to an even grander egress where her mother was waiting.

The driver called out to Jonnie, "Wait here. I go bring key."

Glancing around the vast compound, Jonnie noticed overgrown ivy that skulked along the lifeless flowerbeds beside the house, and scaled up bleached brick to dangle loose leafy arms. The green thinned around the rectangular windows, as if someone had recently taken shears to them. Jonnie took a deep breath, feeling easy in the garden's peaceful glow. It reminded him of paradise depicted in religious pamphlets at the market. Blissful, and teeming with glee, he imagined Margaret's smile as he described the garden to her. He saw her laughing too, with a baby at her breast—a girl perhaps, with soft eyes like Margaret.

The driver's raspy voice came from a second-floor veranda. "Bright?"

"Yes, sah?" Jonnie answered, squinting from the sun's glare.

The other man tossed down keys. "Grass cutter *dey* inside store."

WALKING AROUND THE FIELD mowing the lawn, Jonnie maintained his smile, thinking about how much he would earn from the day's work. They had yet to discuss his fee, and his mind ran freely to the amount of money the woman would pay. How much would he request? Was there a set rate for gardeners? He did not know. Whatever it was, he hoped Margaret would be proud and greet him with a smile.

Jonnie held the large scissors in one hand, pausing to trim the busy ivy with every other step. Nearing the window to his left, he found his arms were too short to reach. After moving the ladder over by about two feet, he climbed up again. This time, he stopped in front of the window. The leaves were thinner there, hanging like fringes above the pane. He cut them, revealing the clear glass. On the other side, covered in flowery pink sheets, a bed sat in the center of the room. Jonnie peeked into the window and saw the woman's daughter, face-down at her desk. She raised her head. Jonnie ducked. She rose and began undressing. Jonnie climbed back down the ladder.

After restoring the tools inside the storage shed and locking it, Jonnie noticed the rake left outside. The driver made a sudden appearance. Jonnie picked up the rake; his heart drumming with fear as the man silently stared at him. The driver looked around the yard. Sweating profusely, Jonnie kept a firm stance with his fingers wrapped tightly around the handle.

"Madam *wan* see you," said the driver.

"She *wan* make I come inside?"

"*Abi* you *wan* make she come outside for you?"

Jonnie chuckled. "Ah, no sah. I *go go* inside."

A quake gurgled inside Jonnie. It traveled down his chest, tightened his stomach, and incited that shaky dance in his knees that often signaled *run!* But he also knew it was time for atonement.

"Go inside," the driver repeated. "Madam *dey* wait."

"Yes, sah," Jonnie answered, and he let the rake slip gently from his grip.

At the front door, Jonnie scraped his feet on the mat before stepping inside. The tiled floor was cool to touch—as if he were resting his calloused feet in a bucket of water. A breeze streamed freely from the air conditioner above his head, and the matching sofas resembled cushioned arms waiting to envelop him. A television flashed the faces of women in a choir as gospel music floated from a loudspeaker. The smell of fried fish and chips and freshly sliced oranges surpassed the easiness of that parlor and all of its luxurious furnishings. Jonnie stepped around one of the sofas with his hands in his pockets. "Yes, mah?"

The mother was at the head of the dining table. Her daughter sat in silence to her right, shoving morsels of fried potatoes into her mouth, alternating with sips from a Coca-Cola bottle. The woman waved Jonnie closer. Jonnie's feet grew heavy, deadened to the respite of the tiled floors.

"Do you know why I called you here?" the woman asked.

Jonnie glanced over at the girl. "No, mah."

The woman leaned back in her chair. Jonnie held a firm gaze on her, feeling tugged on by the daughter's awkward silence. He finally dropped his head and said, "Sorry, mah."

"For what?"

Jonnie looked at the daughter again.

The mother said, "She is not staring at you. She is blind."

"Mah?"

"You keep looking at her. She is blind."

Jonnie exhaled. "*Abeg*, forgive, mah. I no know."

"I called you in to ask if you mind doing all the work."

"Yes, mah. I like plenty mah, but—"

She held up her hand. "I saw you every day walking around with that sign. But today, you looked better—happier. And God told me to invite you in."

Jonnie raised his head purposefully. "He did?"

"Strongly."

Jonnie's eyes watered.

"Do you have a place to live?"

His hand wavered as he attempted to hold back tears. "So-so."

"We need a gardener and housekeeper. You can live in the boy's quarters instead of your so-so housing."

Jonnie raised the hem of his singlet over his eyes.

She paid him, and Jonnie prostrated. "Ah, yes, mah. God bless you, mah. *Tank* you, mah." He rose off the floor, hesitated, then asked, "Madam, *ehm*, no vex, *abeg*. I get pregnant wife. She fit come?"

"Can she cook?"

"The best, mah."

"Bring her tomorrow, and we can see."

THE BUS ROCKED WILDLY on the pit-infested roads outside Ikoyi. Lulled by the rhythm, Jonnie saw himself with the sun on his back, trimming tangled ivy, shaping the hedges, and raking up leaves as Margaret looked on with smiling eyes, and their children carried on in the compound. Of all the things the girl could have been, blind was not one he considered. He had never been more pleased by someone else's misfortune. When he began to laugh, he felt it shooting out of him with persistence, and he knew Margaret would laugh too when she heard the story.

At home, Jonnie tapped against the wooden door to Margaret's room. He heard a murmur and turned the knob. Inside, he gently placed a bag of Margaret's favorite chocolate cubes beside her head. His heat surrounded her. She stirred, fluttering her eyes wide. In a whisper, she wept. "Jonnie?"

"I wake you? Sorry, *o*."

She yawned. "No problem. You come back?"

"Yes, Margaret. *Abeg*, no vex *wit* me. I no go beat you again. I get plenty work today. The madam come say we fit live for *dem* boy's *kuttas*. You, me, baby *sef*."

Margaret sat up with stern eyes while Jonnie fumbled with a matchbox and candles. In the light he carried near her, she forced a smile as she blinked off tears. "Oh God, Jonnie."

"Yes, Margaret, we *tank* God."

She palmed her forehead as he sat beside her.

"*Shay* you *don chop*?"

"No, *o*. I sleep since morning."

Jonnie counted some of the money, and gave her the greater portion. "Save *dis* one. I *go go* buy *akara* and *dodo*."

She seized his wrist before he could leave. They locked eyes.

"Jonnie, I wan tell you say—"

He cupped her cheek. "*Wetin?*"

She wondered if she looked different to him. "Jonnie, you no vex *wit* me?"

"For *wetin?*"

"*Ehm*, the *ting wey* I say?"

He smiled. "No, Margaret. I no vex." He knelt. "Love no be small *ting, o.*" After separating her hand from his wrist, he kissed her and wiped tears off the corners of her eyes. "Make I go buy food," he whispered. "You and my *pikin* no go hungry again." He had never smiled with so much freedom.

"Okay," said Margaret as she watched Jonnie step out of the doorway.

Lying down, she kept a hand against her abdomen and pulled on air. Her head was too heavy to lift. Freeing her breaths allowed the pain to pass, but it always returned. She stared at the bin in the corner, remembering what Mr. Singh had told her. The second tablet would take away the discomfort and flush out the problem. Should she forget or change her mind, he had shown her pictures of what to expect: a baby with limbs melded with its torso and eyes where its mouth ought to be, one born as a puddle of skin and bones, and another with a head too small for its body. Her fingers tunneled through rubbish until she pinched the tablet. As her insides grew taut and loose, and goosebumps rippled on her skin, Margaret called upon the same God that seemed to always help Jonnie find his way. Then she swallowed the pill with a full cup of water.

LATER, WHEN JONNIE RETURNED, he unraveled the newspapers filled with fried bean cakes and plantains. Margaret came in after him.

"Where you go?" he asked.

"I go toilet. My stomach *dey* pain me, *sha*," she answered.

He placed a hand to her forehead. "*Nah* because you *no chop* today. Sit down, eat."

She knelt before the spread of food and pressed a bean cake into her mouth. Jonnie asked, "*Shay* the pain *don* finish?"

Margaret pictured the blood-soaked underwear she tossed into the gutter and said, "Yes, Jonnie. No more trouble."

THE BRIDE PRICE

THE RAINS HAD COME and gone, and the earth was sweaty beneath the scorching Sudanese sky. The women came out to the measured call of the first drum. One foot led the other in sync, equally decorated at the ankles with rings of shells and sharpened twigs. Bodies swayed gently, wrapped from top to floor in their colorful *toub* that flowed in the settling wind. Heads were adorned with crowns of braided hair, cowrie beads, and feathers from fertile birds. Feet quickened feverishly to the sounds of a pending celebration.

One head was bare, smooth from the razor's trip around her skull just moments before. They called her *Ma'a*, the word for water, for all the rain that accompanied her birth. Ma'a followed as the elders split a path to the center of the field, though she wished only to see more of the dancers.

The darkness ahead hung high, pulling dread from its deepest lair. Ma'a's heart thrashed inside its cage like caught mackerel, yet her lips spilled no distress.

Grandmother spoke. "Come along, show your worth."

The words slipped into and gonged around her head. Trusting the mouth of an elder whose worth was exhibited similarly long ago, Ma'a stepped forward. The formerly lonesome drum merged with others to strike a beat that flowed into the heavens. When the sound returned to earth, it awakened a dance among the women and their voices hummed in unison. The matriarch stood to sing, and the women's bodies shook as if fire took hold of their feet.

Ma'a wanted to empty her mind of its fear. All she had ever seen lied between the untamed Red Sea and the surreptitious gardens outside her village. Spread behind the horizon was a world far beyond her grasp—Ma'a hoped to see it one day. That, however, required traveling some unknown journey—one she could not fathom no matter how hard she squeezed the thoughts in. Before she allowed her mind to carry away the noise, a pinch at her side snatched her from the distraction. She moved her feet. As if suddenly empowered by the unknown, she pictured all that was good: warmth from the night air, rain fresh from its seasonal break, and food for the way it made her feel complete.

"Show your worth," she whispered to herself. "Go in there and lie down. It will soon be over."

A pair of old freckled hands led Ma'a into the tent. Inside the cabin of stretched goat hide and reinforced branches from Arabica trees, Ma'a spotted a bed of dried and woven banana leaves. She let her knees lead her to the floor before twirling onto her backside. As if descending upon her, eyes as hollow as the blackness of night blinked above her petrified body. Hidden behind the glare of mothers and daughters of great-grandmothers was blatant camaraderie and hopes of another smooth transition.

The earth grew loose inside Ma'a's grip. Indeed, she spread her callow legs, and another duo of even more mature hands placed the sharpened metal between them before severing the evil that lured so many to sin. Ma'a screamed. Warmth began to travel down her split, slowly. Thrashing about, she cursed them, those mothers and grandmothers, and she swore at the dirt as it drank her blood.

Four pairs of hands pinned her limbs against the ground as

the remaining flesh was sliced off in one brazen swipe. Two more available palms cupped her mouth, trapping the cries of a child en route to womanhood.

"Do not scream anymore! Your younger ones are listening," said the grandmother in a voice as coarse as the withered leaves beneath Ma'a's bleeding bottom.

The severity of pain as that special skin split from her body was unexpected, even with all nine years of preparation. She called upon death—saw it as the only gate from that hell.

"Please come for me," she cried, again and again until her screams dwindled into soft whispers of defeat.

As the oldest hands sealed the hole with what felt like thorns, Ma'a implored the universe for relief. The wound was then anointed with a mixture of oils and herbs. Chants reverberated from all of them, but the bitterness of Ma'a's lament overrode their song. With her eyes shut, she imagined herself gifted with the freedom of birds that glide in the sky when the sun is highest and said, "If only I were one of you."

When night fell, the tears and pain did not retreat as her mother promised, and Ma'a felt cheated once more. By morning, the sky ripped the blackness off its chest and trees raised their heads to the sun. A rush of hot water filled a basin, and Ma'a reached in with a cloth.

"Soon, a husband will come for you," said the timid voice inside her head—but she swatted at it, as she had the flies that circled her meals.

Days in, and the spikes inside her wound tempted her to scratch. Ma'a picked at the patch of leaves and cloth, hoping to find her missing flesh behind the folds. Each time she glanced between her legs, there was more blood. Lulled dormant by the sight of all that red, a dream invited her into its timeless wonder. She heard voices gurgling, and the jerking pull of her waist this way and that rocked her deeply. In her dream, she found herself in the secret garden, a meeting place for the souls of lost children.

"It is beautiful here," she said, to the grand palms and endless array of fruit trees. Rooted in a line, they led her to the eternal quarters of children like her brother, who had never grown past his first breath, children like her sister, who never returned after being cut, and all the other children whose bones were set in a maze of human ways.

Clear water beneath the white-faced moon carried life up the stream, and Ma'a stepped into her namesake. The breath of the woods kissed her skin as she floated in the warmth of the night. She feasted on honey and berries, and placed her body flat against the earth until droplets of rain landed on her one by one.

Waking from her slumber was like traveling at unnatural speeds. Rain fell upon the roof like soldiers marching. Time blew in and out of view. Numbness bolted her hips to the floor and she screamed to rid her body of the pain. To run through the silver lines that stitched earth to sky is all she wanted, but for the pain. When a hand on her head peeled wide her eyes and poured in a fiery light, the sounds around slipped away.

LATER, MA'A EMERGED FROM darkness to the thuds of her head bobbing against a floating bed. Her eyes followed the moon and the stars that winked above the trees ahead. Unfamiliar language planted itself inside her ears, whispering, "You will be all right. You are going to a hospital."

There, the screaming cut through her days like wind through trees. The scent of blood and fermented flesh unfurled in the air and bodies of more moaning girls arrived on makeshift beds and shabby trucks.

Ma'a felt the stubble on her head and reached between her legs. A pillow filled the void where the pain had subsided. She smiled, remembering the way those women danced and sang to her as she entered that hut.

At the end of forty days, she would be seen as a woman, back in her village. Boys would no longer be permitted to frolic in the fields of knee-high grass with her, and men would come for negoti-ations. Once chosen, her body would belong to her husband for as long as she lived, and her hole would be reopened for him and his babies when the time came. It was the price one paid to be wife and mother, she thought—a price that might be worth it one day. But until then, Ma'a chose to rest.

In her dream, she danced like rain. She raced through the fields of bone and grass, and rinsed her body in the warm night air. Sitting inside the arms of the river, she watched birds soaring back and forth as freely as the sky is wide.

NOBODY'S CHILD

JOSEPHINE STARED AT THE baby through a stream of tears, tracing a finger around her eyes and lips. The little brown thing squirmed and stretched in its newness, swaddled in pink. When she released a low din of a cry, Josephine withdrew her touch. A nurse pored over Josephine with a face of fat and pallor and a pensive frown. "You okay?"

Josephine glanced at the woman, then away.

"Anyone coming for you in the morning?"

Josephine shook her head and swept away tears. "No. No one."

The nurse began massaging Josephine's left shoulder with sincere solidarity. "It's okay. Is there no father?"

Any response would only embolden the nurse's compassion and despondent eyes; her pessimistic grin and the kneading of Josephine's shoulder. So, Josephine admitted, while smiling over her daughter, "She is mine alone."

"That's the right attitude," said the nurse, before moving into another question. "Did you have her picture taken?"

"They say one hour."

With words pinched and slow, the nurse asked, "Does your baby have an outfit? We have plenty extra."

Josephine rolled her eyes. Was her age—seventeen—a factor in the question? Was her blackness? She pointed to a leather duffel bag strapped to a chair.

The nurse dragged her words slowly. "You want me to get something out of there for you?"

"The nylon bag inside, please."

She held it up. "This?"

"Yes."

After placing the sleepy-eyed baby in the bassinet beside her bed, Josephine removed the layette from the bag and spread it over her right thigh. The yellow one-piece was not shiny. It did not boast current cartoon characters. It did not say *Mommy* or *Daddy's Girl*. However, it had led Josephine to joyful tears when she first saw it resting in a bin of donated clothes at Flower Child. The outfit, so blatantly neutral, seemed to approve of her choice to wait to discover the baby's sex. She had smiled and wept with delight as she folded it neatly inside the hospital bag days before labor began.

When the nurse asked if Josephine knew to wash the clothes before first wear, Josephine replied, "I got it from Flower Child. Already clean."

With contrived finesse, the nurse moved to the sink to wash her hands. Through vigorous scrubbing, she said, "You have to wash donated clothes first, you know?"

Josephine chuckled. "Just a joke."

The nurse's expression was blank. "I will stop by for your baby's temp check later."

While her daughter slept, Josephine could not sever her gaze. *Let me see those eyes, girl.* She searched for pieces of herself in all of the child's features, wondering how much she had given—how similar the two of them would be, how long her lenient curls would stay. In a daze of slow-mounting fatigue, she pictured her own mother, who often praised the similarities in their elongated legs, their dimples, their heart-shaped lips. She also remembered how, the last time their eyes met, anger was the only thing connecting them. Words had volleyed between them—one blaming the other for why they found themselves on the verge of motherhood, grand-mother-hood, and dishonor. Josephine's mother, whose Nigerian accent added heft to her words, was outspoken. She had yelled into the telephone, as if reporting a crime, "This girl has gotten herself pregnant under my roof. At only seventeen, *ehn*? She needs to come in for abortion, now, now!" The shouting carried on until she was told Josephine would make the final decision. Josephine's feelings mattered too.

"Feelings?" her mother roared. "There is no room for feelings. You cannot embarrass me and our whole family like this. Over my dead body will you have a baby. You will abort or get out of my house." She hung up.

Josephine made her choice then: to keep her baby. After moving through homeless shelters, she found her luck in a letter. A roof, finally. Mother or no mother, family or no family, Josephine belonged to someone else now, and it was time to begin the living part of their lives.

At the start of this new life, Josephine was awakened by a gentle nudge against her shoulder. "I need to check your blood pressure, honey," said the nurse. Josephine sat up and gave the nurse her arm. She glanced over to the partition where her neighbor's family filled the room with a slight racket and enough blue balloons to darken the space. Josephine glanced back at the blood pressure cuff, feeling tears trickle down her cheeks.

The nurse asked, "Why are you crying, honey?"

Josephine shrugged.

"I was a single mother too," said the nurse. "You'll be all right." She handed the baby to Josephine. "Tia is a lovely name."

"Thank you."

Whispering, the nurse added, "Some men are just never ready to grow up."

Josephine wanted to tell the nurse that her tears did not come due to the lack of visitors in that stark recovery room. She wanted to say she did not require the voices, flowers, balloons. The tears, as they came, were a betrayal, a false reading of her emotion. Either they flowed autonomously or were somehow controlled by the slow drip attached to her wrist. She did not know. She knew only that she was ecstatic to be a mother. So, she shrugged her shoulders again, deciding the nurse did not deserve an explanation for the silence surrounding her and her child.

An hour later, a woman with dreadlocks swept up in a scarf came in with neatly-stacked papers in her hands. Josephine eyed the tattoo of an *ankh* on the woman's inner left wrist. She had two small cowrie shells dangling from her ears, and some in her hair. The green, black, and yellow colors of the Jamaican flag showed on her sleeves beneath her scrubs. The woman smelled sweetly of amber oil, countering the sterile scent of rubbing alcohol in the air. Josephine sat up when the nurse told her it was time to order the birth certificate and social security number. She set the baby aside in the basinet and listened to the woman's fluid directions. She was pleased they were coming from someone who looked like her—brown, black, American—and proud of her African heritage as she hoped her daughter would be. At the end of the instructions, the nurse asked Josephine if she was from Liberia or Ghana. "I can always tell just by looking at a person which part of Africa they from."

Josephine waited, wondering if it was the broad nose or high cheekbones or rounded forehead that revealed a person's nationality. When the nurse did not say, Josephine submitted, "I am Nigerian."

Patting her chest, the nurse said, "Ooh! I've dated Nigerian men."

Josephine said, "Oh."

The nurse whispered, "I got all the womanizers, girl." She cackled like a tormented hen and tapped Josephine on the wrist.

Josephine responded with an equally erratic chortle, having learned since moving to America that with strangers, it was better to feign understanding. Like when she took her first bite of pizza, and did not bother to ask what the stringy white substance was on top of the pie. She had decided it looked like scrambled eggs and swallowed with a smile when it tasted like oil and salt on dough.

The nurse held her pen ready. "What is your child's name?"

"Tia Maryann Thomas."

Looking up, she paused, believing her accent betrayed her. She repeated the names, stretching them even, "Tee-yaa … Mah-ree-ann … Tuh-mus."

Hanging stagnant eyes down at Josephine, the nurse asked, "No Nigerian name?"

Josephine replied, "She is American."

The nurse tilted her head, rolled her eyes, and shrugged. Josephine reciprocated the gestures. She was reminded of one of those women who considered themselves *conscious*—more aware of how to be black. It was annoying—insufferable. They let their hair go matted, and sang *peace* and *love* whenever Josephine walked past them at the Ashby flea market. She would answer with a *hi* and feel foolish while fumbling through a series of smiles and nods.

After recording the name, the nurse asked about the baby's father. Josephine said, "Unknown." Then she signed the document. It was done. Tia would always be American, with many more options than Josephine had, and a mother who would not discard her at the sight of imperfection, she promised her daughter.

"Thank you, God," she whispered. And as she nursed Tia to sleep, she quietly sang His praise:

Baba, ose o

Ose o Baba

Baba, ose o

Ose

The following morning, the nurse helped plug Tia's seat inside a taxi. Josephine climbed in beside her daughter. The nurse said, "Peace, my sister."

Fondly smiling, Josephine replied, "Goodbye."

It was December 1992. Rain dragged on for weeks. It was the heaviest winter Oakland had seen in recent memory, and colder than Josephine had ever experienced. The energy required to heat her apartment ate away one hundred sixty dollars from her paltry budget. Wrapped in dread, her hands trembled as she entered the telephone number and waited through the ringing.

"Hello?"

"Mummy, it's me, Josephine." She coughed, almost losing the pronunciation of her own name in the phlegm.

"Yes? This is Ronke."

"I have delivered, mah."

"And?"

"*Mo bi obirin*. Her name is Tia."

Her mother was silent.

Josephine repeated, "I said I had a girl, her name is—"

"I am on my way to work. I will call you back tonight."

Josephine felt heavy inside as she hung up. Night came and went, three times over. The heft in her chest began to swell. By week two, it had grown so much and pounded so loudly that her ribcage felt too small to contain it. The third week in, it finally burst. Josephine bolted out of sleep, wanting only for the mass inside her core to die. Hands on her chest she muttered, "Breathe, breathe, breathe." When that would not quiet the storm within, the words *kneel* and *pray* came to mind; so, she knelt and her words rose out of her until the panic lulled.

Opening her eyes to a new day, Josephine sighed with relief that she was still here, and that Tia slumbered quietly in the bassinet. She looked over at the unpaid electric bill, and climbed out of bed. The clock sat with a blank face. The lamp would not enliven. In the bathroom's vanity mirror, Josephine faced more defiance from the bulbs and screamed into a folded towel.

She sorted items in the refrigerator before discarding the fish pie and bean porridge. Inside the freezer, between the meat and vegetables, she placed the milk and eggs and pot of okra stew. After finishing a pint of ice cream, she sat inside her despair, picking cookie bits out of her teeth. Begging was not disgraceful if the need was real, she told herself, remembering a bumper sticker she once saw that read, *yes is your friend, but no is not the end.*

With Tia slung across her chest, she stood in a phone booth through six stretched rings. Clouds of frost left her lips. "Mummy, please—they cut my lights. Can you help me?"

Ronke answered, "I did not help you make that baby. Do not call me to help raise it."

In line at the resource center, Josephine swayed, rocking Tia to sleep. Her weary gaze swept about the reception area. She watched a pregnant young lady in a taut hoodie holding open the glass door, arguing with someone she could not see. The lady spoke Spanish until her interlocutor entered the building. Then she shouted at him in English, "Fine, you watch 'em, *estupido*, I gotta go stand in line." Waddling in slowly, the lady tousled her hair and followed as the man led a stroller with twin toddlers strapped in. Josephine moved her feet so he could park.

When her name was called, Josephine entered a windowless room and settled opposite a heavyset Latina behind the desk.

"Is your most current electric bill here?"

Josephine pointed to the top of the pile. "Yes."

The woman removed her glasses. "Why did you let it get so high before coming to us?"

"I didn't know, *mahm*."

Leaning back in her chair, she asked Josephine, "Do you work?"

"I receive cash assistance."

"How do you pay your rent?"

"God's grace, *mahm*."

"I need actual numbers, dear. How do you survive?"

Josephine counted on her fingers. "My apartment is housing assistance. I get help from food stamps too—"

"And the baby's father?"

Josephine dropped her gaze. She preferred never to speak of the matter, but there she was, ordered yet again to summon the whereabouts of someone expunged from her memory.

"I do not know," she said, mildly irritated. She might have said it a million times to her mother alone. Now, she swore to it again, with her right hand high. "She is only mine."

"Well, she is not really yours alone," the social worker countered. "I am helping to take care of her. My neighbors are paying for your food, your subsidized housing." She pointed to the door, "Everyone is taking care of you two, with our taxes." With a hand over her heart, she concluded, "If you want some independence, you will get that baby into daycare and get a job. Then you won't need to ask her father or anybody else for help."

Josephine waited at the bus stop under an umbrella. As her tears came, she ran them over with the back of her hand. On the lawn across the street, a sign read: *Mrs. Tran's Daycare, now enrolling*. She scribbled the telephone number into her planner and waited to catch the bus.

((● ● ●))

TIA HATED THE NIGHT. Josephine had come to loathe it herself, and felt anxious after their evening walks. Routine and exercise, the doctor said, would silence the throbbing inside her chest, but nothing in the world was more terrifying than being afraid all the time. Fear had become the only constant in Josephine's days: fear of permanent insomnia; fear of the struggle; fear of unraveling, again.

Some nights, Josephine could get away with just singing Tia to sleep. At times, Tia needed a bubble bath and lotion rubdown, and she would jut her legs when the soft bristles of a brush ran across her scalp. Wrapped in the yellow that complimented her russet skin, Tia would then nurse and fall into a milk-loaded stupor—much in the way those Johnson and Johnson commercials promised motherhood would be.

On the night the sky cracked open for the second unraveling, Tia was asleep. Josephine had washed the dishes and cleaned up toys. After sipping hot tea from beginning to end, she decided to take a bath: a slow, quiet bath without regard to cleansing. But it was then, just as the water began to settle her soul, that the baby girl announced her presence.

At first, Josephine questioned having heard a sound muffled by the door between them, and she stretched her neck to hear. She wrapped herself in a robe, only to be met by silence. Back in the tub, she waited. Her shoulders remained tense, and warmth would not restore itself across her body. She waited for Tia's crisp, sharp cry. When it came, it moved itself clear across their studio apartment, declaring that all was wrong in the world. *Mother! Fix it, fix it, fix it!*

Dripping in soapy water, Josephine picked Tia up and rocked her. She sat, she stood, she sang. She walked in circles until dizziness slowed her. She stared at a bare wall, defeated. She had heard that this worked: ignoring to conquer. Baby accepted the challenge. Steadily, Tia's crying took shape, mounting from low to thunderous. The jutting of her legs was no longer due to pleasure. Sweat gathered on her scalp. Sweat gathered on both of their faces. Josephine stared out the window as her daughter screamed and the metal bars appeared impassable. Mothering should not be this difficult. The urge to leave should not be this strong—but she wished to go outside where it was quiet, where it was calm. A mother ought not to abandon her child, she knew, but she was surviving without hers, wasn't she? The sky had not collapsed when she had to go it alone. The world continued its spin.

However, when it broke open that night, the sky had also poured out more darkness than Josephine had ever known. As the urge to silence her baby dragged her to the steps of total disentanglement, a place no mother can ever come back from, Josephine placed her baby on the bed and left the room. On the other side of the door, she planted an ear against the wood and hoped for silence. The lower the crying became, the softer the thumps in her chest. Mother and child had room now—room to sob separately until fatigue conquered agony. On one side, Tia had fallen asleep. On the other, Josephine gazed stoically at a cold bath.

When Josephine returned to Tia, the baby had kicked her blanket loose and found comfort in suckling one of its corners. Josephine saw her daughter's enflamed face and saturated curls and felt her own panic return. After stifling the rising dread with a forced heavy breath, she cradled her baby and cried, "I am so sorry. I am so sorry."

Babies cry. That baby was only doing what was most instinctive, said one of the neighbors when Josephine apologized for the boisterous night. The older woman walked over and stood close enough to share the air.

"Have dinner with me. Bring yourself and Baby and we can be alive together under the moon."

SMOKY LAVENDER COATED THE air in the woman's apartment. From inside her embrace came a breath of neroli oil. There were lit candles in all four corners of the sitting room for an ambience that pressed Josephine's voice into a whisper. She introduced herself to the baby. "My name is Flora. What is yours?" Amid the soft drumming emanating through a pair of speakers, Josephine took the cue to speak in sugary patois, "Me name Tia."

Flora's head shook until a smile flowered behind her censure. "Talk to her as you would with me. Baby talk slows language development." She laid a hand over her heart. "I'm a teacher—twenty years now, and we're always learning new things."

Josephine nodded and smiled.

Beaming, Flora urged, "Come in. Sit, sit. I am so pleased to finally have you over."

"Thank you."

Josephine sat on one of the floor pillows surrounding a zebra-print rug.

Flora seemed to float from room to room, humming in all directions. Her wide-hemmed skirt trailed her walk, and Josephine thought the woman would trip and fall each time she rose off the floor. When she returned with a tray of foods, she named all of the items: "Cashews, pitted dates, dried banana chips, olives, hummus, pita bread and, of course, freshly sliced apples."

Josephine reached across the platter to grab a cashew, believing the buffet of snacks was dinner.

Flora chuckled. "You can have more than one."

The two of them picked at the board, nibbling in silence, awaiting a nexus to an interesting topic. Flora bobbed her head to the music, and asked of the performer, "Do you know him?"

Josephine answered, "I don't think so. My parents only listened to church music."

"Where are you from?"

"Nigeria."

"So is he. Fela Kuti?"

"Oh, yes. We came when I was nine, but I don't know this song."

Flora nodded. "No wonder your accent vacillates. Mind if I ask how old you are now?"

"Eighteen."

Flora's eyes caught light when shifting, so Josephine added, "Almost."

Flora smiled. "Babies come to us when they come."

"Tell my mum that," said Josephine, immediately regretting her candor.

Flora sang, "Don't hold your head in shame for the way life happened to you."

Josephine nodded, but her head still hung low. When she looked up, Flora was in tears. Her lips quaked and liquid dribbled from her small, pink nose.

"What's wrong, Flora?"

"I get a little emotional, I'm sorry." She gathered her bearings with two deep breaths. "Uh, are you in touch with Tia's father?"

"No. The baby is just mine."

Flora cupped both of her eyes with her hands and said, "Oh my God." She shook her head vigorously. "You too?"

"I don't know what you mean."

Flora moved over to a bookshelf near the kitchen door. She lifted a framed image of a little boy in a three-piece suit, bow tie, and tilted beret. She handed it to Josephine. The warm sepia tone of the picture suggested it was taken long ago, and Josephine asked if the camera used was one of those bulky ones that left a plume of smoke after each flash.

Flora nodded. "That's exactly right—it is vintage."

"Who is this?" inquired Josephine.

"Handsome, right?"

Josephine bowed. How else does one respond?

"My father as a young man. He was one of the 'good coloreds,' my grandparents would say. Not that they would choose him for their daughter over a white alternative, but he was at least light enough to give my mother a child who could 'pass.'"

Josephine did not know what to do with this information. She stared at Flora's mouth with foisted courtesy, hoping Tia would drop one of her tearful bombs.

"Could you tell I was black just by looking at me, Josephine?"

Josephine shrugged.

"I know I don't look it, but, the one drop rule says I am." Her arms upstretched to the heavens. "And I claim it!"

"In Nigeria, you would be considered half-caste." As Josephine spoke, she felt the hand of confidence at her back. "But people would think you are a white woman, and kids would sing about you in the streets."

Flora sat closer, "Yes. Now, isn't that sad? We don't even know our own people because color blinds us." She shook her head. "So sad."

It was sad not to have food. It was sad to sit in darkness because money did not behave. It was sad to be abandoned by one's family. Sadness was not to be summoned on a whim, to sit and soak in. Sadness was the consequence of real hardships, not something like one's race—at least not when Flora's hue would allow privileges Josephine would never enjoy. But, dutifully, she nodded, agreeing that racial ambiguity had informed the melancholy in Flora's life. She felt relieved by the smile on her neighbor's face.

While Josephine pressed her nipple into Tia's latch, Flora watched and cheered. Imploring Josephine's pardon, Flora ran into the kitchen and drew the partition shut. In an uncertain moment, the racket sounded like Flora was being attacked by the contents of the utensil drawer. Josephine chuckled, deciding the woman had finally tripped on her long skirt.

When Flora returned, she knelt on the same zebra skin where they had shared appetizers, and placed down a trivet and a *tajine*. She lifted the lid of the pot to expose couscous drenched in a stew of mixed vegetables. Josephine stared at the food, wondering if meat was tucked underneath.

"I forgot something," said Flora.

When she returned with a bottle of white wine, Josephine watched her serve herself.

"Want some?"

Josephine shook her head, no.

"Oh, I hope you don't mind. I don't eat meat."

"No problem."

"Nigerians do, right?"

Josephine thought of the animal carcasses in her freezer and replied, "Sometimes."

"I don't know any Nigerian cooking, but I hope Moroccan is close enough."

"It's no problem, really. Thank you."

"Maybe you can teach me to cook your food if this interview goes well?"

"Interview?"

"I'm joking. You know, how all dates are interviews to gain relationships?"

"Oh, I see." She did not.

Josephine surprised herself by how much she ate, even though she had planned to feign a stomachache and escape. She delighted in how much they laughed, and how much more enjoyable she found Flora's eccentricities after wine. She even shared her concern over the tray of snacks, and the commotion in the kitchen. Flora cupped her mouth to seal in laughter. They followed the meal with what Flora called vegan bean pie, and Josephine admitted that while she enjoyed the dessert, she preferred animal products in her foods. Flora laughed heartily, and swallowed more wine, and smiled with glassy eyes. "Thanks for sharing your evening with me, Josephine."

"Thanks for inviting me."

"When was the last time anyone asked you how you felt?" Flora asked, sitting closer to Josephine as she spoke. Josephine searched her thoughts, shrugged. Flora said, "Well, no matter what you're feeling, know that the bad will always pass, but so will the good."

Josephine nodded.

Flora raised a hand to smooth the top of Tia's head as she slept in the sling on Josephine's chest. "She doesn't look much like you. Is her dad Nigerian?"

Josephine answered truthfully for the first time. "No, he is not."

"Or American? Sorry. I guess he could be whatever. Are you two involved?"

Josephine's mind wandered to when lust, the worst of transgressions—according to her mother—first stirred her. Her mother noticed it too. She warned Josephine, "At fifteen, boys should not be on your mind." But they had been. Avoiding them was like trying to breathe through her ears. If a boy smiled at her, she imagined his kiss. If one touched her, she played naked images of him in her mind. She listened to music only in her Walkman's headphones to hide the salacious lyrics that now enticed her. When she discovered her fingers had the power to draw out an itch that boys were not permitted near, she started spending more time alone. Amid one of her tremors, she vanished inside the sweet rhythm cast throughout her body. When she opened her eyes, her mother poured a pitcher of cold water on her head. She dragged Josephine to sit before her father until she was ready to explain why she sinned this way. After, the three of them prayed for God's hand to lead.

Flora broke Josephine's concentrated energy. "Come back."

Josephine answered, "Oh, sorry."

"I asked if her father sees her?"

"Tia is God's baby," said Josephine.

Laughter fell out of Flora's mouth. A line crawled onto Josephine's brow.

Flora said, "Oh, you're not joking?"

Josephine stood. "Thank you for the dinner." She grabbed her diaper bag hastily and kept a hand on Tia's back as she headed for the door.

"I'm sorry, Josephine. I was insensitive."

Josephine paused, stiff-eyed. Her words slid between her teeth, "She is mine because God gave her to me, full stop."

"I can understand that."

A hand on the doorknob, Josephine added, "You need to mind your own business."

Flora stood next to her and whispered, "You're right. You don't have to tell anyone anything you don't want."

"I know. Goodbye."

IN THE MORNING, A note slid across the floor into Josephine's apartment. It read:

Be happy. Be scared. Be angry.

Be brave even when you don't want to be. Be funny.

Laugh because it feels good. Be honest. Be kind. Be present.

Be strong. Be weak. Be mother. Be sister. Be friend. Just be.

Always with love, Flora

While Josephine was busy being, she found herself in a middle place: neither good nor bad. A housekeeping job kept the lights on and food on the table. Parenting classes bleached out the darkness of anxiety. Tia's cry lost its sharp edge and became a lenient blend of giggles and babbling. Josephine realized then that the sharpness in her baby's cries had been honing her, preparing her for the gift of hearing her new name: *Mama*. Next came "Mama I'm hungry," "Mama, play," and "Mama, I love you." When Tia started walking, Josephine crouched with her arms extended for Tia to enter, and it was exactly as she had pictured motherhood.

MOTHERING FLOWED EFFORTLESSLY UNTIL Josephine was hurled into Tia's terrible second year. Then, rearing a child was work and only work—from when the sun dangled in the sky to when it rolled back into night. She never got to tell Tia stories from her childhood, though she tried many times to share the one about why snakes now slithered on their bellies. She seldom got past the first line: *Long ago, snakes walked upright like you and me— some so tall, they touched the sky.* Something else always required her attention. Without another person to lean on, Josephine found herself again wondering if single motherhood was worth it. Between years three and four, Tia threw tantrums over sleeping, waking, eating, drinking, bathing, going to and leaving the park, with high-pitched screams that Josephine had no choice but to silence with spankings. In her fifth year, Tia had learned to seal her mother's ire with smiles, and obedience—and during that time, Josephine did not feel inclined to shout, or hit, or cry after hitting. Together they lived in that place—just being—and there they stayed for another year.

In their new apartment amid the perpetual vivacity of North Oakland, Tia had her own bedroom and Josephine had hers, and sleeping was easy. Life streamed from day to day auspiciously.

Mother and child strolled toward the bus stop in the day's aching heat. They passed a decrepit Victorian house spitting out its loud dancehall reggae across a brown lawn while an agitated German shepherd sprinted back and forth behind a chain-link fence. Josephine veered from the canine's warning into the street. An old man shouted, "Mornin'," from the porch. Josephine waved, pushing Tia along. The man crushed his cigarette beneath his army boot, blew out smoke and said, "Y'all have a nice day, now."

Josephine's body hardened whenever they passed that house. The constriction altered how words left her mouth—and she sensed that Tia could feel that tension, too, when Tia squeezed her hand as if waiting for the stiffening to pass. When Josephine's words softened again, Tia sought the peace in her mother's eyes with a smile.

Josephine's smile carried over to the bus stop, and she waved her pass as they stepped up. Tia parked herself in the seat behind the driver and Josephine stood holding the metal bar above her head. The bus rocked into transit. After a few blocks, an older man wearing a *dashiki* and tie-up trousers climbed in. His silver dread-locks hung to the back of his knees. He sat across from Tia and rested his hair in his lap. Tia stared at him until she heard coins clanking through the machine.

Josephine looked over at the woman paying, trying to remember where she had last seen that face. When the woman spoke, Josephine remembered seeing her pregnant and waddling into the resource center with a man and twins in a stroller. Six years had changed nothing about the woman's demeanor, and she used the same raspy, overcooked voice to urge a boy Tia's age onto the bus.

"Move," she yelled, shoving him up the aisle. She got off the bus and returned carrying a stroller with a sleeping infant wrapped in a green blanket. The mother sat beside the old man and placed the boy's hand on the stroller's handle. He folded his fingers around the plastic grip but they slipped off when the bus accelerated.

The mother snapped, "I said hold on."

Josephine watched the boy struggle to remedy his blunder while his other hand latched on to a rubber Power Rangers action

figure. At the next stop, his fingers loosened from the stroller. The
mother slapped him on the head and commanded his silence with
a hand raised near his mouth. His next slip drew a gasp out of Tia.

"I said, hold on to the goddamn stroller," said the mother,
ripping the toy from his hand and tossing it out the window.

The boy's screams filled the bus. "Shut up," the mother yelled.

Grumbles from the other passengers rippled from back to front.
The old man shook his head. By the time the bus reached Solano
Avenue, the air was filled with tumult. Strangers threw harsh
words at the young mother, and she returned them. She rolled her
eyes, adjusted and readjusted herself. "This my child," she kept
saying, as the boy stood drenched in tears, pointing at the window.

At the next stop, Josephine rose quietly and led Tia off the bus.

"Welcome to Mrs. Tran's." The highly caffeinated Vietnamese
woman greeted them with the same words she had used to
welcome them every morning. Josephine kissed Tia goodbye, and
took the bus back downtown for work.

THAT NIGHT, A SHARP wailing sound woke Josephine. It was
not Tia's cry, and it could not be the tremors next to Josephine's
heart—that angst had gone mute for a couple of years now. She
lied awake pondering the incident on the bus. On behalf of that
boy and his mother, Josephine felt an unsettling culpability for
having witnessed their interaction. Kneeling, she tugged on God's
ears, begging Him to watch over that mother and son, strangers
who had passed through her life and left something behind. It
wasn't the first time, though, was it?

She watched television mindlessly. When that wouldn't help,
she climbed in bed with Tia, basking in the child's tranquility. Her
fingers traced Tia's chubby cheeks and amber skin. She compared
her daughter's slack curls to an aunt she once knew, blamed the
tawny hue on the summer sun and swimming in chlorine. She
pulled back Tia's bangs until her eyes slanted at the corners.
Awakened by the pressure, Tia stared back.

"Mommy, who is my daddy?"

Tia had asked before, and would ask again, Josephine knew. To say she had pressed him too deep into the shadows of her mind to remember, or to claim God, would no longer suffice. The truth would come forward, as it is wont to do. The discarded memory had grown hands and clawed at her, digging for a way out of its entombment.

Josephine remembered her arms had gone up in jubilation when her mother said yes. She had arrived at that party with friends, who one by one trailed off into dark rooms. The neon lights bounced off the walls to dancehall reggae and she wound her body until sweat melted into a smooth sheen on her skin. A hand cradled her waist. She remembered its breadth, its strong grip. She saw his eyes, and shut hers—not knowing she would be different the next time she opened them. She tasted his salty mouth, swallowed his scent, felt the tender pinch from his fingers inside her skirt. "You have to say yes," he said. She complied, and there, pressed against the wall, she had called out, *Oh God. Oh God. Oh God.*

When the party was over and light consumed the shadows, she rifled through the crowd for his hands and eyes and hunted his scent. Throughout her pregnancy, she studied the face of every man she met. She wouldn't see his eyes again until she held her daughter in that hospital bed. She knew then, that one day the child would ask. What Josephine would not know how to relay was the fact that darkness had poured over her and injected forever inside her womb, and when the veil was lifted, nobody was there.

Faced with the question, she saw the time had come to be brave, and vulnerable, and honest—all the things Flora had listed in her note. "I don't know," Josephine spat.

Tia said, "Okay," and returned to sleep.

Josephine stood before her bathroom mirror and cried until her tears dried in a salty trail. Her fingers ran across the stripes left on her abdomen and breasts, and the shame woven into them. She became angry with herself for believing God prevails—for believing in God at all. Her stomach churned, and she felt herself shrinking inside humiliation for telling her story as if she was Mary, and God had chosen her to bear His child. Silently, she cursed God for allowing life to happen to her that way.

JOSEPHINE STARED FORLORNLY AT her daughter as they ate breakfast. She rushed when sliding on Tia's sandals, and on their walk to the bus stop, she pocketed her hands when Tia reached for them. Along the way, she ignored the neighbor's salutation, his dancehall music, the dog, the heat. On the bus, Josephine seized Tia by the wrist when she dawdled. Tia rubbed the point on her arm where Josephine had pressed firmly into her skin. Josephine stared at the floor for the duration of the ride while Tia sat tearfully beside her. All was quiet. When she looked up at the man across from her, he glared back.

The push uphill to Mrs. Tran's house was wrapped in silence.

Tia pressed the doorbell.

"Welcome to Mrs. Tran's."

Josephine knelt with outstretched arms. Tia cautiously entered her mother's embrace. After a long squeeze, Josephine left a kiss across Tia's cheek. Tia went in. Josephine walked back downhill just in time to meet her bus.

WHEN TIA TURNED FIFTEEN and mouthy, she sometimes forgot whose womb had cradled her—whose blood fed the cells that formed the mouth she used to shout at her mother: *Bitch. Liar. Slut.* Josephine ended the insults with an open palm, and ignored the tears. She delivered one of many final warnings: "I am your mother. You will never disrespect me."

When Tia was born, Josephine had counted the features she had given her without regard to the parts unseen—the areas one cannot compare until it is too late. The troubled teen years, Josephine would cast as a passing phase, like a traffic jam on the highway. Tia's exodus would soon come, said mothers who had waded through the same swamp of adolescent angst. Be patient. After entering college, an unfurling would take place inside Tia's chest, just like it had with her mother—only she could not quiet this internal dread with breathing or praying. She would try to drown it in wine coolers, smother its verve with marijuana, slice into her skin to help it escape. At twenty, she would seek a way out of that darkness, and ask once more, "Who is my father?" Josephine would relay again that the truth had only eyes and fingers and a voice that echoed off the walls between pleasure and pain. When that would not do, she would shout, "Stop asking. I don't know." To fill the hole left behind, Tia dragged faceless men inside that chasm until it was someone else's turn to call her Mama. On and on it went, until someone decided to step out of that cycle. When the telephone rang one day, the ending began with an apology.

"Hello Josephine. This is your mother."

IN HER SHOES

I RUN IN THE mornings. I keep my head down to ignore the elderly couple walking their poodle. When I look up, the sun is fixed atop the plum trees ahead, welcoming me to the end of my run. I slow down, gather my breath. "Wow," I whisper, as clouds bow out of view. Light tumbles over a field of fog and dew-laden grass. My shoes are covered in mist. Had I the promise of seeing that sunrise again, I would have done exactly that with the rest of my day.

I check my phone. Over an hour has been eaten away. There is a missed call from my aunt, but no message.

Warm water pleasantly beats against my skin in the shower. It reminds me of when I first came to America—how infatuated I was with freshly delivered hot water. It further amazed me to see my aunt's bathtub in a room of its own. She had told me to take a hot bath. I inquired about where she kept the pots.

"Why?" she asked. Her eyes lingered above a knowing smile.

"To boil water for my bath."

At least she had not laughed. In the bathroom, she introduced me to what I still consider the best thing about America: hot water spilling from the faucet without all the fuss of gathering wood or losing kerosene too soon. In Lagos, a small bucketful would have sufficed for bathing. I feared draining my aunt's world of its abundance of warmed water, and turned it off. She extended permission through the door. "Fill the tub, take your time." I could hear her smile from the other side.

I undressed as water carried steam on its back and plunged into the blanket of bubbles. Suds around my ankles awakened the pores all over my body. I sat and stared at the dripping faucet. *This is why Americans are so happy*, I told myself.

Now, as I am showering, the phone is buzzing again. It is her. She always tries three times in a row. First, she would complain about never hearing from me, with all the intended guilt. "What if someone is calling to say I was shot?" she would say. I overlooked the second attempt. By the third, I habitually answered with, "I was just going to phone you."

The ringing stops. I mutter to myself, "Why doesn't she just text me?"

Instead, she leaves a message with four succinct words: "*Mama e ti ku.*"

I drop the phone on the floor and stare at it. I wait for more details to climb out of the speaker like ants from a mound. There is only silence. Within the unnerving quiet, I feel my blood fighting the slow pace of her words swirling round my head, "Your mum is dead."

On the wall, I see ten years of wasted time in degrees that never inspired pride in my mother's eyes.

"Finish high school, and university," my aunt had asked of me. "Then you can go visit your mum." She had also said, "But only if you go unscathed." I didn't understand this until she clarified.

"Imagine your virtue is one million dollars sitting in a clear bag. It is strapped to your back for everyone to see. Some will try and take it from you. Others will sweet talk you. But only you can choose when and who to share it with." I nodded, unsure of what she meant, but obedient.

The next time my mother had called, I asked her to explain the bag story. She enlightened me. "Do not open your legs for anyone, full stop."

"Why didn't Aunty just tell me that?"

"Aduke," said my mother, "my sister is just that way."

My aunt's indirect way of speaking appeared when she lingered around the kitchen during my conversations with my mother. She hovered closely with her gaping smile, urging me to share my contentment for life in Berkeley. There were too many apprehensions to share, especially since my mother was spending a fortune to call all the way from Lagos. Instead, I leaned against the wall where the telephone hung loosely from its jack. "I like living here," I finally said.

My aunt snatched the receiver. Giddily, she spoke in an ironically fashioned American accent. "Did you hear that, Soon-bow? Your daughter lost her Nigerian accent already." I looked forward to when she would correctly pronounce my mother's name: Soon-*buh*.

As I walked away, I heard my aunt say, "Thank God. I never trust sending money to Nigeria, *o*." I was halfway up the stairs when she reverted to speaking Yoruba. She complained about her children. "They never call or visit … one day police will call them to report my death."

After the phone conversation, she went to her bedroom and sobbed, loud enough to snag my attention. I knocked on the door. "Aunty, what's wrong?"

"Your mum," she began, when I sat on the chair beside her bed.

My stomach tightened to the worst thoughts. Cancer? Malaria?

She sat up. "Your mum is lucky to have you. I hear how much you love each other."

I exhaled.

"I wish my children brightened up that way when we talk. They always sound inconvenienced—"

I knew then I was locked in a rant that was likely to last beyond the end of *The Arsenio Hall Show*. Her complaints were American: *My coworker is trying to destroy me. The gardener missed some weeds. The cable is out. My feelings don't matter. I'm fat. I need a bigger house. I need to downsize. People only want my money. No one ever calls. My children never call. My children only call for money.*

I lent her my ears for as long as she needed. After, I returned to my room and stared at the pictures of the children she spoke of so vaguely— children who were out conquering the world, children who had forgotten their mother. I saw that as the only real problem in her life, and I grew saddened by the thought of my own mother weeping over my absence.

The next morning, I begged my aunt to let me go back to Lagos—not permanently—during spring break or summer. Dread sat on her face like an extra set of eyes. She asked me to finish high school first. After that, UC Berkeley wrecked her pocketbook. "In due time," she had promised, all those years ago.

That was then. Now, when I finally call my aunt back after getting the bad news, neither one of us knows what to do with the heavy stillness between us. She does not mention her own death or a fear of mine, and could not speak of her sister.

"I got your message," I say.

"I am so sorry, darling. Let's go to the funeral together."

AT SFO, WE HUG. She stares into my eyes intensely. Hers are glossy, as if she would start weeping at any moment. Mine, I hope, appear more composed.

I say, "It's okay, Aunty. Let's go."

She loosens and retightens her *iro*, briefly exposing a slip underneath the wrap. Her eggplant-colored ensemble is made of sheer lace. Sparkling buttons fill the eyes of the flowers scattered in the design. She is also wearing a *buba*—a blouse with funnel-shaped sleeves and rhinestones gaudier than her ostentatious wrap. I want to ask why she didn't just throw on a pair of jeans and a collared white shirt, like me. She is Nigerian enough, anyone could tell by looking at her.

At the ticket counter, the loud thud of her purse startles the woman who offered us assistance. The woman smiles and asks for our tickets and passports. Soon, my aunt is arguing with her about the weight of her luggage, though the scale flashes fifty-five pounds.

"No more than fifty pounds, or pay extra," the woman says, still smiling.

My aunt shouts, "No. I prefer to remove some things."

I watch the struggle between my sixty-year-old aunt and the bag filled with god-knows-what for a weeklong trip. She bends over, huffing and cursing in Yoruba, as if anyone but me understands. After I pay the extra charge, my aunt says, "Don't waste your money."

"It's no bother," I say. I only want to escape the gawks and sniggers of people who do not know that my aunt is simply that way.

Finally boarding the plane, I sigh with relief. Squirming in her seat, my aunt asks, "Are you okay?"

I fiddle around inside my purse. "Yes."

"It's just the two of us left now, isn't it?"

I shrug.

"My only sister, gone. You have no siblings, and my children insist the world is overpopulated—so it's the end of the road as we know it, right?"

I nod.

With her back to the window, she says, "It is all that terrible Lagos driving. I wish I had bought my sister a car, so she wasn't walking everywhere."

Softly, I reply, "Aunty, I can't do this right now."

She nods. "I know. When my mother passed, I didn't want to hear it. I was in London. I thought Sunbo was calling to tell me she delivered you when she said *Mami* died. My heart dropped."

I nod.

She continues. "You were born days after the funeral. I told her to name you Yetunde, to honor losing our matriarch." She pauses. "Aduke suits you, though."

I lower my sunglasses over my eyes.

"Okay, I see I am bothering you. I'll be here when you are ready."

The cabin quiets, as people plug into their individual realms of music and movies and books. I order a drink. Across the aisle, an Asian woman in her fifties leans over to me and whispers, "You very pretty."

I smile.

My aunt peers from around me, "Thank you. She is my niece." She nudges me, "Say thank you."

At twenty-five, I don't enjoy getting told to mind my manners. But I say, "Thank you," with a smile, exposing all my teeth.

I shut my eyes and tilt back my head. My mother's smile flashes across my mind, leading me to a place I'd rather avoid. What happens to a body when a car flings it in the air and it lands with bones askew? Was her skull fragmented? Did she die instantly? Did she suffer? I try to focus on seeing her alive instead. A tray of goods rests on her head. She is shuffling her feet as she walks. I see her sandals. I see her feet. I see relief in her eyes when she knows she is home for the night.

My aunt has drifted off to sleep. She mutters between snores. When she awakens, I ask, "Are you okay?" She blinks repeatedly as if she does not understand my Yoruba. I repeat, "*Se e wa?*"

"Fine, yes," She answers. "Why?"

"Just now, you were talking in your sleep."

Confusion enlivens the wrinkles in her brow. "I was?"

I draw a sip from my cocktail and say, "Yes. You were thrashing about."

"*Ah ahn,* me? And they did not pull the plane over?" She shrugs.

A handsome flight attendant drifts near, offering to refresh our drinks. He says, "I just love your eyebrows." I thank him, submitting willfully that the arches on my forehead came by the hands of my esthetician. When he returns with twice the gin, my aunt declares, "He's flirting with you."

"No."

"If you didn't follow this trendy natural hair nonsense, he might ask you."

I laugh. "Aunty, how many men ask about your eyebrows?"

Her eyes wander. "Plenty of men, all the time." She lies.

"How many of them wanted to sleep with other men?"

She cups her mouth, whispers, "He's not gay." She looks at him. "Is he?"

I sip my gin and tonic. She asks if I drink often.

"Sometimes."

"Aduke," she cries, sharply. "You don't want to become alcoholic, you know."

I wag my finger. "There are worse things to be."

Another call for the flight attendant, and another drink arrives. My aunt requests water with her eyes locked on the Bible. Unbothered, I pour the drink into my mouth. I am beyond the warmth of a gentle buzz. My aunt is trapped in her seat. I loosen the buttons of my shirt. "The reason I don't call is—" I begin, before stopping to take another sip.

She fingers some lines in her book, mouthing the words.

I continue, "I feel like—"

She throws up her hand. "I am praying." Her eyes are shut.

I say, "When the missionaries arrived, the African had the land and the missionaries had the Bible. They taught us to pray with our eyes closed. When we opened our eyes, they had the land and we had the Bible."

"What are you doing, Aduke? I don't tell you about your alcohol."

"Jomo Kenyatta said that, not me."

"Aduke, don't be rude."

I turn over, stare at my iPad as my aunt plugs into her Bible.

Neither of us speak. Another drink leaves me slumped over in my seat.

The scent of bergamot surrounds me when I fully open my eyes. It reminds me of when my mother boiled tea in the mornings.

"Did you sleep well?" my aunt asks.

I stare ahead. "Fine."

"They are serving food."

"I just need two Tylenols," I say.

She shrugs. "It's all that alcohol."

"That's okay." I search my purse.

"No one wants to marry an alcoholic, you know."

"I am not—"

"A man wants someone virtuous, smart, beautiful …"

"I don't care what a man wants. I unloaded that bag years ago."

She shakes her head. "Well, that's a shame."

"It's not."

"Have you been exercising, taking your meds?"

"I run every day," I answer—though I want to say, "You're not my mother." Many times, that phrase has tried to escape my lips, but never as much as today.

"It helps your anxiety, you know."

"I am fine."

My aunt declares, "Well, you have sunglasses at least, to hide the red."

I hum, breathe, focus my thoughts on seeing Lagos again. I imagine the pride on my mother's face before remembering that she is dead. She is dead.

She is dead.

I think it should have been my mother's house sitting on that tree-lined street back in Berkeley, her smiles greeting my successes, her lessons guiding me into womanhood. I see that visa lottery letter arriving. I see my mother dancing barefoot with it in her hands. I see her waving wildly as I cross through the security gates. My heart sinks into my stomach as it did then, when Lagos disappeared into the night, but I remember thinking I would see her again. I feel nothing until I hear myself shout, "You're not my mother."

My aunt pauses from sipping her tea. "Excuse me?"

I sigh, place a hand on my forehead. "You. Are. Not. My. Mother."

She replies, "Are you having another panic attack?"

"Fuck no!" My voice draws attention.

She whispers in English, "Aduke, calm down."

Flatly, I say, "You are not my mother."

"How dare you!" she hisses.

I slap her, shout back, "How dare *you!*"

Her eyes steel in shock. I rub my temple and turn soft with my words, "Oh God. I am so sorry." She trembles. I take her hand. "Sorry, Aunty."

"I tried my best, you know," she cries. "That is all."

The attendant asks, "Everything okay here?"

My aunt raises her hand, "We're fine."

After the attendant leaves, I breathe until I feel calm, and begin telling my aunt about the day I got my job. "I didn't know who to call first—you or my mother. When I called her, she asked if I would visit soon. She was so happy when I said, 'In six months, I'll come home.' Then she asked if she could tell you that I got a job. I couldn't break her heart by saying I had called you first. She sounded so happy, like it was our thing. But you had taken that from us too."

"Aduke, I am sorry. Please breathe."

I sigh. "I was this close to touching her again. This close."

Water wells up in her eyes. She bites her bottom lip, but it still shakes. "Forgive me, Aduke. You are all I have."

I breathe in and out, and wrap my arms around her. I have never been able to watch her cry.

Outside the airport in Lagos, I inhale. I do not remember the city being so pungent with odor—so dusty, so dull. The slow turning sun also slipped my mind. It is too hot for eight in the evening. People cast their eyes on me—some men wink. I purchase meat pies from a glass cart. My aunt begs, "You shouldn't trust everybody's sanitary habits, Aduke."

I offer her a bite of pie, and she accepts.

IT IS THE NEXT morning. Two men show us to a cold room. My mother is in an open casket. I keep my hands at my sides. She is wearing white and her eyes are shut. I am unprepared for her sallow skin, her stillness, the way her wrists cross her stomach. Her feet are trapped in white heels. I am reminded of how she sighed with relief when removing her shoes at the end of each day. Gently, I unstrap the heels and toss them on the floor.

During the funeral, my aunt wails and throws herself against the floor. She begs God to take her instead. I help her up, console her. I whisper *amen* when breaks in prayer call for it. All the while, I have been unable to escape the jarring sight of my mother's body in a box.

After the funeral, I visit our old neighborhood. The door to the room I once shared with my mother is narrower than I recall. I pull the cord attached to a ceiling bulb. Light spills over all she possessed in the world. It is like being in my dreams, feeling swathed in her presence but unable to touch her. I lie on her threadbare mattress and let my tears sink into the pillow. Her old sandals peer at me from beneath the cupboard.

My aunt enters the room with a man. He bids me a lenient greeting in English, "You are welcome." I sit up and nod. He asks if I still speak Yoruba. I answer, *"Be ni."*

He laughs heartily. "Thank God. Never forget."

They discuss the past-due rent for my mother's room.

My aunt asks, "Aduke, what should we do with her belongings?"

I shrug my shoulders—forgetting that while it means "I don't know" in America, Nigerians see "I don't care." I say in English, "I only want her shoes."

SNOW BY MORNING

IT WAS A PART of town I did not know. Mother, Brother, and I climbed out of a taxi, and dragged our bags across the plank over the gutter. We trudged through a garden of mud and rocks before entering the building. At the top floor, Mother rattled the cast-iron bars. A lanky, bare-headed girl scurried out.

"Good afternoon, mah."

Mother told her who we were, and that we were there to see Nydia. After a nod and a kneel, the girl unlatched the deadbolt, sorted through the keys at her waist to undo the padlock, and finally drew the heavy gate ajar.

We sat on the bench in the corridor of their flat after the girl excused herself to fetch her madam. I saw light pouring through the French doors that led to the veranda at the end of the corridor. Mother and Brother rested their bags on the floor; mine remained in my lap. Madam Nydia glided toward us in a *kaba* that reached mid-calf. In its looseness, it hid the shape of her body. Her arms went up. She emitted a croaky greeting before hugging Mother. Brother prostrated. I knelt. The cold tile pressed into my knees. I quickly rose off the floor. She tapped Brother's shoulder. "Stand up, please."

The girl had been standing with her face down and hands clasped beside the chain of keys. When the madam's fingers danced in the air, the girl looked up, nodded and disappeared behind a curtain into the kitchen.

"This way, please," urged the madam, again with that commanding hand.

I reached for my bag.

"Leave it."

Mother and I flinched.

Madam Nydia waved me forward. "No one will bother it."

The three of us followed her into the parlor. There were two parallel sofas, a glass coffee table, and a standing fan—but the television stood out for its imposing position inside the entertainment center, with all its wires sweeping in and out of the other boxes. I sat beside Mother. Brother boxed me in. Madam Nydia sat across from us.

"How old are you?" she asked Brother.

"Seventeen, mah."

I sang out. "I'm eleven."

She looked sternly at me and I knew I had spoken out of turn. Facing my brother, she continued, "Do you want to watch film?"

He nodded.

She walked over to the television, pressed the corner of a tinted glass door that revealed several rows of video cassettes. The names of the recordings were handwritten on the sides of the cardboard sleeves.

"Have your pick," she offered.

Brother chose one that read *music awards*.

"That's not a film, it is just a music show with singers—but you are welcome."

Brother inserted the cartridge into a VCR and pressed play. I stared at the screen, seeing Michael Jackson in color for the first time. My smile widened and I held my hands up, ready to applaud when his feet slide gracefully across the stage. Brother firmed his brows at me. I stilled myself, quieting the elation that nearly poured out of me. I loved Michael Jackson, and hoped to meet him one day. He was in America, where Mother is from—where we were headed to. Although I was born in Chicago, I had lived in Nigeria with Father's family since I was a year old. It was Mother's people's turn, Mother told us. But Brother had divulged to me that our parents were getting divorced.

I did not believe him.

On the ride in to Madam Nydia's home, I had asked Mother if she and Father were getting divorced. I needed to hear it from her.

Mother spat, "Of course not."

"Will we see Daddy again?"

"Yes." The trip was not an end, she said, but an opportunity not to be missed—Madam Nydia was paying our way to America. "Everything is fine, baby."

Mother then told me we were going to Chicago to see my sister—the one she had said I resembled, the one who in pictures had caramel skin and long hair and eyes like a cat's. Between us was an overnight flight, and by morning I would awaken to a new sibling, and stark white snow.

While we were watching television, the house-girl brought in a tray with three Cokes, one Fanta, and some biscuits. She placed the snacks on the coffee table. I immediately reached for the orange drink. Mother told me to pour it into the tumbler, as if she had foreseen my intent to enclose my lips around the bottle's spout. I nodded, filled the glass and sipped slowly, hoping to remedy my blunder.

"Oge," said the madam. "Bring another Fanta."

I crumbled biscuits on my tongue and flushed them away in one big gulp. I wanted to be prepared for when Oge returned with my second Fanta. When she did, a man followed her in. Madam Nydia called him darling, and Mother's face brightened at the sight of him. She said, "Hey, hey now," before hugging him. He shook

Brother's hand and I noticed his nails were long like a woman's. He shot me a wink. The three adults chattered loudly for a few minutes until an infant's cry drew the madam out of the room.

The man sat, asked Brother if he played football. Yes, said Brother, he loved it. I loved it too, I interjected. "And I play too." The man then wanted to know why a pretty girl like me was kicking a ball around with boys, and he asked Mother why she allowed it. Brother answered first, insisting I was an excellent goalkeeper, adding that they called me "spider girl" because of my long limbs. Mother shrugged. She had not known that I played with the boys.

The man eyed the scars on my legs and told Mother, "You have a tomboy on your hands."

She chuckled and altered her American accent to sound more Nigerian. "Yes, that is *hah*. Neighbors children are all boys. No *gurls*."

"Is that all her hair?"

Mother fingered the braid resting on my shoulder. "I cannot stop it from growing, *o*."

"Well, she will break someone's heart one day."

"Thank you," I answered, as I always did to such things, especially if Mother was near.

No one else seemed interested in the Fanta sweating in front of me, so I stretched forward, hoping to reach it before anyone noticed. The madam came in just then, and her hand swept over my head to grab it. She handed the bottle to the man, "Open this for me, darling." He lifted the bottle to his mouth and pried open the cap with his canines. The madam sat beside him with their son who was not an infant, as I had presumed from his cry. He sat upright on her lap and pointed to the bottle in the man's possession. She took the bottle and placed it to the baby's lips. He pulled on it like a straw and his parents chuckled. Brother chuckled. Mother laughed. I feigned amusement, with a hand over my mouth.

The man told Mother the football playing explained why my legs were ruined. Mother nodded, as if she did not remember that the spots came from mosquito bites when we spent Christmas at

Father's village in Badagry. When he suggested we ask the madam for a cream she used to lighten her skin, Mother smiled and continued to nod. Did she actually forget she abhorred skin bleaching?

Madam Nydia spoke up. "I don't *bleash, o*. I am fair complexion."

I splayed my legs, studied them, and was about to open my mouth when Mother tapped my knee and whispered, "Close your legs."

I pulled my dress back over my knees and turned to the television.

"Oge," the madam shouted.

The girl arrived out of breath, as if expecting to meet an emergency. Madam Nydia asked for the baby's bottle.

"I am boiling the water now," Oge responded.

"So? What are you still doing here?"

"Yes, mah," the girl answered, before she lowered her head and shuffled hastily out.

The baby giggled and blew spit bubbles and clapped his hands. I smiled at him.

"You wanna hold him?" Mother asked me, returning to her usual way of speaking.

"No."

Mother released a nervous laugh. "She's good with babies— good good—real nurturing." She was talking about me. She must have forgotten I was the same girl who ran away after church when asked to mind the toddler room. She did not remember that babies crying made me cry too. She had let it lapse that when she told me where babies came from, I had fainted.

Seeing Mother's face stiffen, I went to the madam and reached for the baby. He came to me with ease. His skin felt like clouds had been deposited underneath. The top row of his teeth was black like his curly hair, and he smiled with his eyes. He pressed his head against my chest and dripped spittle on me. I knew to smile through it, though. Oge returned to take him to her hip, and left to feed him.

I felt the drinks moving through me and asked for the latrine. The madam shouted again, "Oge."

Oge returned, breathing heavily with the baby at her hip. "Yes, mah."

"Take her to toilet."

"I can wait," I said. "No problem."

Mother chimed in. "I'll take her. Where is it?"

"Out of the flat to the end of the corridor and to your right."

Oge said to me, "Sorry, mah."

I answered, "It's okay, thank you. My mum will show me."

The cast-iron gate squeaked under its own weight as we passed through. I was not expecting its abrasive shriek when it slammed shut. I flinched and grabbed Mother's arm. She pulled me close. "Everything is fine, baby."

Trekking down the dark hall that parted rooms on each side of us, I asked her, "Mum, why did that girl call me *mah*?"

She shrugged.

"Does she think I am older?"

"It's just out of respect, 'cause she's the housegirl. She's probably older than you—sixteen or seventeen—I don't know. She's just little. You remember how small the people were in your daddy's village?"

I nodded, though unsure I ever noticed.

"But she doesn't wear a bra. All the girls in my class already need bras."

"Everybody's different."

After taking a right turn at the end of the hall, Mother pushed open a door. It was dark in there, and green slime spread across the floor and up the walls. A basin for water was pressed into the corner.

"That's the bathroom," said Mother. "Maybe this other room is the toilet."

The second door was a closet with a cracked porcelain bowl covered in fecal matter. The odor reminded me of when the septic gutter was being emptied in our neighborhood. I shook my head. Mother shoved me. "Go on in there, I'll watch the door."

When I came out, Mother was gone. I called out, "Mum?"

A man standing nearby pointed back the way we had come. I entered the tunnel-like corridor and called again, "Mum?" Again and again, I called out for her until I reached the gate. Oge let me in.

"Where's my mum?" I asked, cross and loud.

Oge shrugged.

I stormed into the parlor and Mother was sitting beside Brother.

"You left me," I said, in the same tone I had used with Oge.

"I knew you could find your way back."

"Oh," I said, but it angered me still. I wanted to tell her so, but we didn't do that sort of thing, share hurt feelings with a parent. I crossed my arms on my chest. Madam Nydia stared at me long and hauntingly, sending a chill to my core. I sat up, uncrossed my arms, and relaxed my face. When the madam turned her eyes onto Mother, they were lenient again, and the room was silent.

Michael Jackson had left the screen and Whitney Houston was begging someone to dance with her. Brother pressed fast forward through her song. The man told us to enjoy the videos, and the madam and Mother followed him to the big bedroom. We heard their voices carrying on with laughter and garbled conversations, and the girl ran in and out with beers.

We watched videos for hours and I began wondering why negotiations for free airfare took so long. After we had seen all the music videos, Brother inserted a film that began with a woman's exposed breasts. He asked me to turn away. I flipped from my back to my side on the sofa and moments later fell asleep.

THE CACKLING OF MY sister's laughter ravaged my dream. She embraced me, as I knew she would, and she asked questions about Lagos—how we lived, and why we were so poor that we needed strangers to give us free tickets to return to America. I answered as Brother had prepared me—by listing all the good in our life. I spoke of how brick and iron surrounded us, and not hardened mud. I told her that windows from the floor to the ceiling opened to a field of grass, green and long. I described our mango trees and their fruit—so much of it that we tired of the nectar, and at times swore off paw-paw because they grew faster than we could eat them. We were not destitute. Outside, a Peugeot 505 belonged to Father, and a grown man drove him around. Another grown man washed that car, and two women washed our clothes. I said it all in the practiced American accent that Brother had also taught me. It was seamless—in my dreams, at least.

I awakened to Muslim prayer outside. *Allahu Akbar.* Brother was sprawled on the floor and Mother was on the sofa across from me.

"Hey, baby," she whispered.

I sent a little wave to her as I yawned. She continued staring at me.

"You fell asleep without eating last night. You hungry?"

I nodded, looking around to find we were still in Nigeria, in the madam's flat, in an area I still did not know.

"When are we going to America?" I asked.

"Come with me," she said.

Brother sat up and leaned his back against the wall. He did not look at me. I followed Mother out of the parlor across the hall to the small bedroom. In there, a chest of drawers, a twin-sized bed, and a bicycle took up the space. My bag was on the bed. Mother shut the door behind us, sat next to my bag, and tapped the spot beside her. She placed an arm around my back and whispered into my ear, "Something came up."

Smiling, I asked, "What?"

"You have to stay here."

I chuckled. "Why?"

"I need you to stay here, okay?" She took my hand in hers. "Until I get back—in a week."

I felt her grip firm around my fingers when I tried to stand. Her eyes lost their jolliness. "Sit with me for a minute."

"Mum, why?" I begged, stretching my words. I could feel my tears falling. "Is Bode staying, too?"

She shook her head slowly. "Your brother is coming with me."

I pulled closer into her hold. "Mum! Please. No."

She kissed my cheek. Her words came out hurried. "I'll fly right back and take you too. They said they would pay for you to go, and now they say they can't. I don't know, baby. Trust me, please."

I took her hands. "Okay. So, just take me back home to Daddy until you get back?"

Her shoulders sank. "I can't do that. I already told him you was coming with me. You know how he gets."

"Please, Mum," I cried, digging deeply for my most convincing plea. "I'll be good."

She kissed my hands. "I need you to be a big girl, now. It's just a week. Just watch television, play with that cute baby, and drink Fanta. You won't even notice I'm gone."

She dropped my hands. I turned to see my bag on the bed. I stood up and shouted, "No."

She said, as firmly as I had ever heard it: "Cut that shit out."

I grew dizzy, eyeing the drawers, the bicycle, the door, the mirror, the walls, the window, the ceiling—and suddenly fell to the floor.

"Don't start that now," she spat. "You ain't no little kid no more. Get up and stop it."

When she left the room, I walked over to the window and stared out. The bodies outside moved customarily back and forth, as if the world remained intact even as mine fell apart. Moments later, Mother knocked on the door, startling me. She asked to enter, as if the choice were mine.

"The car is ready," she told me. "Come say goodbye to us."

I hugged Brother. He still avoided my eyes, but managed to

squeeze out a solemn, "Bye, Spider." They stepped through the gate and Mother waved before their silhouettes turned down the stairwell. From over the veranda, I watched them trek back through the garden of mud and rocks, over the gutter's bridge and into the man's car. Up until the vehicle drove off, and even after, I hoped it had been one of Mother's yarns, and that the car would return, and Mother would remove her jovial mask and raise her hand up for me to come down. But my week had already begun.

When my tears crusted against my cheeks, I went back inside to the parlor, picked out *The Goonies*, and inserted it into the player. I curled my body on the sofa. The American children on the screen went about happily, hunting treasures. Oge came in. She asked if I needed anything. I shrugged. She left.

The gate squeaked open and shut. I heard footsteps. Someone popped their gum in sync with their walking. The door to the parlor opened, and in came the madam. "Are you still sad?" she asked, with concern spread across her face.

"Yes."

"You will miss your mum?"

I nodded.

"So, you are lying here because you are sad?"

"Yes."

"Come, give me hug."

I stood up, wrapped my arms around her, and sobbed into her bosom. She pulled back and smeared the spittle with her hand. Then she slapped my face. I stepped back, and ducked behind my hands. While she was shouting at me in a language I did not comprehend, I wondered if she had been this person all along or if my action drew it out of her—worse, I feared this version of her had come to stay.

"What have you done today?" She spoke in English. "I left, you were lying down. I return; you are lying down."

I cried, "What should I do?"

"You mean, 'What should I do, mah?'"

"Sorry, mah. What should I do, mah?"

"You are asking me question?"

"No, mah," I said. "I will go and sweep, mah."

In the kitchen, Oge held out a broom. She sat on a stool picking apart leaves in a big bowl. I bent at the knees and ran the broom lazily across the floor.

Oge said, "No, o. That *nah* parlor broom, no be kitchen broom."

I returned to the parlor where the madam was sitting on the sofa with her son while the puppets from *Sesame Street* provided background noise. Moving the broom casually around her feet, I noticed her toes were darker than her hands and face, and I wanted to tell her I knew she was not naturally fair-skinned, the liar that she was.

"Don't sweep me, o," she ordered.

I stood straight. "Yes, mah. I wasn't going to sweep you, I promise."

"You think say you *bettah* pass me? Don't you hear Yoruba?"

"Yes, mah, *mo gbo.*"

"From now on, understand?"

I nodded.

I had never heard so much silence in a kitchen during dinner preparations as there was in the madam's house. Oge washed leaves in a basin without as much as a hum. I quietly sliced and peeled yams. The madam stirred a pot of stew with deadened countenance. The walls were grimy, and charred behind the stove. Not even the flame beneath the pot dared a dance.

At home, in our sun-colored kitchen, Mother would play lively music as a signal for me and Brother and the servants to gather. She wore a red apron and danced about the room as she handed each of us a task. A cigarette often dangled from her lips when she cut up meat, when she stirred the pot, and even when she served us food. The best part of cooking with Mother was when she would extend her hand for mine, and twirl me in a haze of her smoke and her gleaming smile. I always felt like I was gifted with the finest mother in the world.

After Oge picked the leaves and ground the peppers, I placed the sliced yams in a pot of water. The madam spoke directly to me, and I remember the way she said it: *Don't touch inside hands pot my.* She massacred Yoruba—worse than I ever heard it—and I wanted to laugh.

One plate of pounded yam, vegetable-leaf stew, and a piece of meat for each of the girls. For the man, a whole lot more. The baby drank milk made from powder and water, and the madam ate nothing. After the family retreated to the big bedroom, Oge washed dishes in a basin and handed them to me to rinse and put away. Oge swept the kitchen and handed me the mop. Oge spread a mat on the floor inside the small bedroom and offered me the bed.

The first time I ever dreamed of daggers in my chest, I woke up screaming. Mother had come running into my room, and kept my arms steady until I returned to sleep. After that, my nightmares consisted of me tumbling endlessly within an abysmal void. In the madam's house, while I slept, I felt a chill in my scalp, and I heard commotion just before talons tore into my chest. My screams came out muffled in my fight to escape. When I opened my eyes, all was quiet in this part of town I did not know. A shadowy figure hung in the doorway while Oge snored peacefully on the moonlit floor.

Allahu Akbar was the song that woke me in the morning. I knew America was not outside then. There was no snow, and the air smelled too familiar—not foreign, not good. The baby's cry lanced the air, piercing through my disappointment in the dusty perfume of Lagos.

I yawned loudly.

"I pray this baby will sleep again," Oge said to me. "Let us start by boiling water."

Shocked to hear Oge speaking Yoruba, I nodded and climbed out of bed. In the kitchen, she told me her real name was Ikuseghan and I should call her that but never in front of Madam Nydia. I nodded and cast my eyes on the small kerosene stove on the floor. No sense in giving her my name since I was only there for a week.

I would never see any of them again, I thought, though I did not tell her that.

Ikuseghan emptied the steaming kettle into a bucket and lifted it. I followed her through the corridor from one end to the other. She pushed open the door to the dark room, and it pulled me into its fetid hold. After handing me a bar of soap, she showed me where to hang my drying wrapper. When she left, I stood naked with my bare feet on the slimy ground, and smeared the bar all over myself. I washed quickly, draped myself in the cloth, and ran back to the flat with the bucket slapping my legs along the way.

Standing naked before the mirror in the small bedroom, I ached between my legs. I remembered the last time Mother asked to see my body. My hands had not gone up to hide my breasts, and I had not crossed my legs in shame. She glanced at the patch of hair where my thighs met and said, "You didn't tell me you got your hair."

I had shrugged.

She said my sister started at ten, and she hoped I would too.

"Started what?" I asked.

To be a woman, Mother told me, one must bleed each month, and for seven days and nights. Aghast by the thought of losing so much blood for so long, I asked her where it would come from. She pointed between her legs. "Same place your babies will come out of." I gasped.

She said, "Once you start, it'll come every month unless a man puts a baby inside you."

I sighed. "Forever?"

"When you get old, it'll stop."

"Does it happen to Bode and Daddy too?"

She shook her head and said it was a female thing. Women were the source of life, and men, although free from bleeding, were unfortunate in that they would never know the feel of being two in one, of being caressed from inside, of knowing a child before its first breath. "It's called bonding."

I furrowed my brow. "Bonding?"

"Yeah. A deep connection can't nobody come between."

I told her I did not want a bonding or this thing that would start bleeding one day and for seven days and nights, and I certainly did not want a baby to grow in or come out of me. She urged me not to worry, told me to find the nearest woman should she be unavailable. "She'll know what to do." It had been a year since Mother first alerted me to this impending doom of blood and babies, and everyday, I checked, but nothing. As my lower half ached now, I feared the end of my childhood was near.

In the time that I perused my body in the mirror, dressed, and combed my hair, Ikuseghan had bathed herself, dressed, boiled eggs for the baby's meal, and drawn well water for cleaning. She placed a broom at my feet. The parlor needed sweeping. The shelves needed dusting. The corridor needed mopping. When I finished, I wanted to lie back down. I wanted Mother. I wanted Father. I wanted to go home.

"Madam is awake," Ikuseghan warned.

The woman said nothing to either of us when she came out of her room. We bowed. Ikuseghan followed her to the bathroom with a bucket of water and a towel. After she bathed and dressed, the man did the same. The family left in the car. Ikuseghan went to the market. I sat on the bench in the corridor, soaking in the silence of that afternoon.

I tried to recall Father's office telephone number: "943 49 00. No, 943 499 00." I raked through my mind for words Mother might have used with the taxi driver when we first came to the madam. I even attempted to recall anything I saw that would help Father find me—but I could not. Why had our parents sheltered us so much that whole neighborhoods in Lagos were a mystery? I had seen films with witches seizing small children for sacrifice, and heard of kidnappers stealing girls as they walked home from school. Always, I heeded the world's caution: *don't enter a stranger's car, don't pick up money a witch might have left in your path, don't allow ghosts to touch you.* On top of moving cautiously through my days, I never began one without praying.

Now, as I feared I had become one of those lost children, I knew escaping was my only option.

It came to me then to find a policeman, and tell him I had been kidnapped. He would require me to have something for him, I knew, as they all did whenever Father's car was stopped at checkpoint. So, first plan: find something valuable enough to earn the assistance of a policeman. I went into the big bedroom, searched the drawers and cupboards, and stumbled upon an American twenty-dollar bill, and pocketed it.

When I heard the rattling of Ikuseghan's keys, I scampered out of the room and met her at the gate. She emptied her basket. I sat on the floor, my back to the wall. The madam did not like laziness or lounging, Ikuseghan said, or for anyone to disturb her husband. I shrugged my shoulders, told her I was going home soon. "No need to learn the rules."

"What is your name?"

I shrugged.

"I told you mine."

"Okay, my name is Bisola."

She smiled. "Bisola, did you live in a big house?"

"No. A flat."

"Can you talk American-style, like your mama?"

My nose in the air, I nodded. "Yeah."

"Do you know how to play ten-ten?"

I rose off the floor, twirled, clapped, and raised my foot to show I knew. Ikuseghan placed the bundle of keys on the cupboard and asked me to follow her into the corridor. Facing me, she sang, "Ten-ten, ten-ten, ten-ten," and we both lifted our feet. She scored the first point. We carried on and I led for a bit. Then she gathered points by raising her right foot when I least expected. After I lost, we fell over each other, laughing. I felt like the only thing we were required to do was play.

In the evening, the two of us ate rice and hen stew on the floor in the kitchen. She sucked marrow from the bones on her plate,

and then ate the bones. I wrinkled my nose at the whole perfor-
mance, unable to stoop so low.

"You do not like chicken?" she asked.

"I like it."

"Then why is your face doing like so?"

Again, I let my shoulders rise up and down. "I only eat the
meat."

She collected the bones out of my bowl and placed them in
hers.

"We give the bones to our dogs," I said.

"What kind of dog?"

"I don't know. My mum says they are mixed breeds when she
brings them home."

"Oh," she said. "The kind that lives inside the house?"

I pretended not to have heard her.

She went on, "We had a dog when I was a small girl, but he
was an outside one—for barking when people came to our house."

I nodded.

She licked her lips while twirling my bones between her
fingers.

"That dog, we called him Lucky. After we ate *eba* and stew, I
would take the remaining bones to give him. When we did not
have meat, I gave him only *eba*. For a long time, we did not have
bones to give him, and then he started refusing *eba*. I even molded
the *eba* into small balls, and then I made it resemble bones—but he
just looked away.

"One day, my father bought meat again, and I was so happy to
give Lucky the remaining bones. He thought I was bringing only
eba, so I did not blame him for hiding in the back of his cage. I
called him, called him, and he did not come out. I asked my father
why Lucky was hiding, and he told me that Lucky was not hiding.
He pressed my stomach and said, 'Lucky is there.'

"I cried and cried. 'Why, Papa, did we eat Lucky?'

"He asked me, 'Is your *bele* full?'

"I told him, 'Yes.' He told me, 'Food is food.'"

Ikuseghan looked at me when she finished her story. I shook my head; aching in my gut for the dog and for her. She bit the cartilage off the tip of the bone and said, "Maybe hunger never fight your *bele*."

((● ● ●))

WHEN MY EYES OPENED, the song at *Fajr* reminded me I was not yet in America. By the time the midday chorus of *Dhuhr* entered the flat, I had swept and mopped each of the rooms and the corridor. Ikuseghan had fed the baby three times, and I begged her to let me do the fourth so I could sit. Minutes after *Asr* prayer, Ikuseghan shook a bottle of milk near my nose. I sat with my back against the wall on the small bed, and she placed him in my lap. He took food eagerly, and I closed my eyes through the few minutes of rest. At sunset, *Maghrib* prayer began, and I knew the day was nearly done.

On my third night, I had scratched at my arms, fending off claws in my sleep. While I mopped the kitchen floor in the afternoon, the madam stood over me.

"What do you think you are doing?"

"Nothing, mah."

"You are bleeding."

I rubbed my arms. The smudge of blood first startled me, and then angered her. "Go and wash."

"Yes, mah."

I returned in my wrapper and danced naked through midday prayer. A crack in the door, and I thought Allah had come to reprimand me for indecency. The husband's fingernails crept from around the curtain in the doorway. My hand went over the space between my legs, and the other covered my breasts. He did not turn his glance from me, or stumble through his misstep, or turn around to leave. He came near, placed my hands at my sides and called me shy. I stood frozen. He wrapped the tip of my braid around his finger and said I should never worry about being that way with him.

Before Mother had gone, Saturdays were special. She would quarter several frozen chickens before burying them in the oven until they browned, then slather them in barbecue sauce. I liked Saturdays for the feast of roasted birds and mashed potatoes, and the way my fingers smelled of vinegar and spices long after we concluded our meals. I liked Saturdays for the gathering that occurred in front of our small black-and-white television after the longest part of the day was gone. I liked Saturdays for the way my family came together, at least for a night.

Here, Saturday was not for barbecues and films. It was for cleaning and cleaning, and catching a spoon atop my head for not moving quickly. It was for scrubbing the Dettol mix into the linoleum floor faster than my arms could manage, and breathing in fumes until my nose hairs wilted. It was for lugging well water up four flights of stairs with the pail steadily on my head. Saturday was for watching the madam pour bleach into the drinking water and asking me to taste it and laughing when I did. Saturday was for eating leftover stew and rice in the kitchen, alone.

The madam called me into the big bedroom. She spoke in Yoruba, "Has Oge finished washing clothes?"

"No, mah."

"*Lo bu onje fun* Oge."

I pointed to my chest. "Me?"

"No, your twin standing beside you."

I nodded. "Sorry, mah. I will go."

I went into the kitchen to prepare a plate of food for Ikuseghan, as the madam requested. Smiling, I piled the rice high and chose a big piece of meat for her. When I placed the food inside the cupboard, I noticed the madam had forgotten to cover the food she had doled out for her husband. I covered them both and locked the cupboard.

Back in the big bedroom, I knelt at the door and told the madam that I had completed the task.

"What was that?" she asked.

"*Moti bu onje fun* Oge."

"What do you mean, you made Oge's plate of food?"

"Just now, you told me to go and make her plate."

Gingerly, she placed the baby inside his crib and walked over to me coolly. She dragged me into the kitchen by my ear.

"Where is it?"

"In the cupboard, mah."

I heard her shout, "Didn't I tell you not to touch my pot?"

"Yes, mah."

"Why did you touch it?"

"You told me, mah, just now."

"No!" she said. "I said, '*Lo bo onje fun* Oge; go and cover her food."

I braced myself when her hand went up, but I did not expect the sting on my cheek when it came down.

"What did you put inside?"

"Nothing, mah," I swore. "Nothing, mah."

The gate crooned, coarse and long, as the husband entered the flat. He joined us in the kitchen. "What is going on here?"

The madam told him I had poisoned the food.

I shook my head vigorously, shouting, "No, sah. No, sah."

He pulled me upright. I wrapped my arms around him. He whispered, "It's okay. It's okay."

I fumbled my words. "I didn't do what she said I did, I promise."

The madam rested her hands atop her head. "In my own house?"

He said to me, "Don't do it again."

"Is that all," the madam shouted, "for someone trying to poison us?"

They stared at each other. He titled his head. She tilted hers. He turned to face me. "Kneel down."

"Sah?"

"I say kneel down, my friend!"

On my way to the floor, he balled up his right hand and threw his knuckles into my forehead twice. "Idiot! Idiot!"

The husband then turned the back of his hand to me as if he would strike me again. I ducked. He said, "Get out of my sight."

The rest of that evening, I cried in bed before finally falling asleep.

Sunday, the day before Mother was supposed to return, I awakened to *Fajr*, excited to begin my last day there. The baby's colic kept Oge beside him through the night and well after I had bathed and cleaned the flat. Madam Nydia gave me directions to walk to the market, with a stern warning that I must return within the hour. I folded money into the pocket of my dress and raced quickly down the stairs, past the well in that rocky garden, and out into the freedom of the road. The outside air was loose and abundant, and I hoped to inhale enough of it to float away. It reeked too—of grilled meat, smoke, and human sweat. Sewage smells emanated from the gutters, but filled me with delight as I took mouthfuls of the open untethered air. After a week of being prevented from roaming freely, I savored the putrid aromas of my delectable freedom.

It was my first time at a market without the guidance of Mother's arm. While feigning autonomy I shook my head *no* when offered the corpse of a hen for a good, good price. I held the basket in the crook of my arm like an obedient housegirl and kept my mind on the time. I spoke Yoruba to a man selling fish, and greeted a Fulani woman in her *sari*, "*A salaam alaikum.*" Her children smiled at me and stuck their hands out and pointed to their mouths. I used pidgin to score okra and extra peppers for the night's stew, and when the conversation moved toward comfort, I asked the woman, "*Nah* where we *dey?*"

She pulled her wrapper tight. "*Ehn?*"

I repeated the question.

She eyed me up and down. "You no know say we *dey* market?"

"No, mah. I mean which area be *dis?*"

She turned to the person behind her and spoke a language I did not understand. The two of them looked at me and laughed.

In the hour it took to collect groceries, I almost enjoyed the game of give and take with strangers. I had been someone new, someone whose story shapeshifted with each person I met. By the time I finished, I had danced the entire way back, feeling the breeze part for me to pass. At the entrance of the home that was not home, the air steeled again, and I once more became the girl whose mother left her behind. "One more night," I told myself. "Just one."

The madam called out to me in a melodious voice—unlike the barking she usually used to order my presence. When I entered her room, my elation from earlier in the day succumbed to the ache in my stomach. She wrinkled her nose.

Her voice lost its sweetness. "What is that smell?"

I did not know, I told her.

"When did you last wash?"

"*Ale ano*, mah."

"Last night? *Ehn*? Go and wash again before touching anything else. Nonsense."

"Yes, mah."

After my long stay in the bathroom, I returned to the small bedroom and slammed the door. My stomach tightened, and a harrowing pain took me to my knees. My heart would not slow its pace even with measured breaths. Again, I wiped between my legs with the towel to make sure the red was real. I had not imagined my entrance into womanhood happening like this, not with Mother in another country. I stared in the mirror, wondering how to bring the news to Madam Nydia. The mirror showed that I was thin—thinner than before I came there, thinner than when my friends at home teased me for having exposed ribs and sunken cheeks. Dark rings sat around my eyes, as if someone had drawn them in.

"Don't cry," I whispered. "Don't."

When I felt my tears, I hid behind my hands. Wrapped in defeat, I heard the door screech open. The husband came in. He wagged his finger as I reached for cover. "Allow me," he cooed, before covering me in the warmth of his body. He buried his nose in my hair and squeezed my breasts and released a heavy sigh inside my ears. Softly, he spoke, "Your mum will not return tomorrow as planned."

I nodded. "Yes, sah."

"Don't you want to know why?"

I shook my head. "No."

"Well, she left with five thousand of my dollars inside her stomach."

I pictured stacks of money sitting inside her body, wondering how she ingested it all, believing now that they spent all night in that big bedroom feeding her bills like a slot machine to take to America.

He added. "If she doesn't come back, it's your head."

He turned me around, and with his middle finger, traced across my collar, down between my breasts, and toward my navel. He kissed my ear. "And what a pretty head it is."

I mumbled, "*Eje*."

"What?"

I shoved him off. "I am bleeding."

I saw him shudder as if a chill had come over him. He slowly stepped backward until he reached the door. Except for the twinge trailing from my head to my stomach, and the soreness of my breasts, I wished for my first blood to never end.

With only one woman—Madam Nydia—to tell that I had finally entered womanhood, I cried as I asked Ikuseghan to help me tell her. She unraveled a bag filled with tattered cloths and demonstrated usage with hand gestures. After leaving me to pack my underwear with scraps of fabric, she returned with a steaming cup of ginger tea. I do not remember anything else about that night.

In my dream, I saw Mother's silhouette enter the bedroom. She sat on the small bed and rubbed my face. Her hands were soft, and smelled like rain. She asked how I had been. I told her about Ikuseghan's friendship—how Oge was not a name she liked but she was too afraid of Madam Nydia to say so. I described the market, the freedom, the bartering for fish and okra and playing ten-ten with Ikuseghan. Mother massaged my scalp and I felt like I had floated off into space. I told her I found money in the big bedroom, and I had planned to give it to a policeman to take me home, but thank God she came back for me. She did not even scold me for stealing—she only shook her head. I told her how the madam grew angrier each day she found me still in her house. I hated the baby's colic and crying, I said, and cringed when I heard it. It kept me awake, and the exhaustion slowed my hands and feet and caused me to drift off to sleep amid cleaning. The more slowly I worked, the more I felt the madam's wrath by way of her fist, her feet against my back, her belt on my arms. The more the beatings came, the more I wished the madam dead, wished myself dead. I'm sorry, I said, for what I had allowed the man to do to me, how my silence encouraged him to find me while others slept. I had wondered how it would feel to jump off the veranda, and one time I leaned over—but it was as if Ikuseghan had read my mind, and I found her holding onto my shirt. I told Mother I was a woman now, and "Mother, I love you, and I know you love me, and I knew you would come back for me." "Of course," she said, and she leaned in to kiss my forehead before she vanished.

Fajr again. I looked around to find dawn spilling through the window into the room. I heard a loud thud and felt as if the ceiling had collapsed on my head.

"Mother. Mother," I cried, gasping for air.

I could not see her. When I cleared my eyes, the madam and her husband were standing over me. The words exited my mouth liquefied and warm. Red spilled over into my hands. I tried to stand. The madam pushed me back. A second attempt to rise and the madam's hands held me down. I remained still, searching the room for Mother. *Help me. Help me.* But the words hung back inside my throat. I feared my tongue had been removed; there was so much blood. Then, I saw it there, on the floor—my belongings scattered about with the American twenty-dollar bill atop the mound of clothes. My hands went up in supplication. "Sweet God."

Thief, they said. *You will die today.* I tried to get up and the blows came. *Stay down*, I told myself, and still more blows. The man told me to kneel and raise my arms. From that position, I saw them circle me. I felt hot in my face, neck, back, and legs, and parts of my scalp where they had torn out hair from the root.

"Why did you steal?" he asked.

"I don't know."

"You will not get up from there until you tell us," he countered.

Madam Nydia said, "Enough of this spoiling her." She handed him the bicycle chain.

He held it at his side and looked at me with sallow eyes, as if he was tired of beating me. She shoved him in the chest. "Then give it to me." He flogged my back three times. I screamed louder with each lash. She snatched it from him, landed two more strikes before snagging the back of my head. I fell forward.

Hours later, I awakened, surprised to find my head still attached. On hands and knees, I tried to stand. With the help of the bicycle, I propped myself up. I caught a glimpse of my face in the mirror, and the girl I used to be pointed at me and laughed. Outside the small bedroom, I heard Ikuseghan singing. Had I not ached with the pain from a thousand blows, I would have danced. She was sitting on the bench with the baby in her lap. When she looked up at me, she gasped. The baby looked at me and screamed. I returned to the room.

Ikuseghan tied him to her back. She boiled water and washed me with a cloth that felt as if she was peeling the remaining skin off my back. Working hurriedly with her face devoid of expression, she dressed me before placing me back in bed. While feeding me *gari* with milk and sugar, she told me she should have warned me never to steal from them.

"I just want to go home," I cried. "My dad lives in Ikoyi. Please, how far is that from here?"

"This is Ajegunle. I don't know how far Ikoyi is."

"Ajegunle?"

I had heard that word during my parents' arguments. Father called it dangerous, filled with ruffians and crooks. He said that even policemen avoided the area. He had ordered Mother to never go there. I fell further into despair, knowing that my mother had left me in the darkest part of town.

"She is never coming back," I said.

"She will," Ikuseghan countered with promise.

"They will kill me first."

Ikuseghan swore to me. "They are not going to kill you."

"The man said my mum has his money in her stomach. Maybe they killed her for stealing too."

She shook her head and sat beside me on the bed. "They did not kill her."

"What does he mean that there is money in her stomach?"

Ikuseghan rubbed my head. "I have seen plenty people come here and go. They don't carry money in their stomach, they carry something else."

I stared at her, perplexed by her words. "What did my mum carry?"

She mouthed the word *eru*.

"Drugs?"

Ikuseghan nodded.

I knew then Mother was never coming back.

In our yellow kitchen, where Mother baked chicken parts on Saturdays, and spun me around to American music, and her eyes met mine—she had whispered to me, "You my golden ticket." Later on, after the birds were eaten and the television ran the closing credits to *Scarface*, my parents sent us to bed. Their voices began to rise, and the dogs barked, and Mother shouted, "I know what the fuck I'm doing." It got quiet in there. Going to America was not worth a lifetime in jail, Father had said, but Mother ended the conversation with, "I said I got a plan."

While Ikuseghan stroked my head, I asked her if she thought my mother had been caught.

"I no know."

"My mum told me to wait one week and now she is not back, and they will beat me to death."

"Stop it," Ikuseghan spat. "Your life is not the worst."

"What is worse than the way they beat me?" I asked.

Ikuseghan shut her eyes and exhaled. She placed the bowl on the floor at her feet, and her hands went over her scalp. I presumed she was crying by the way she rubbed her eyes.

"My papa," she said, "had four children. Three girls, one boy. One day, he told my senior sister to find work. She did not come back. Then he told the next one, and she did not come back. Then, he said it was my turn because we needed money for my brother's school fees so he can take care of us. This woman is my madam and her husband is my *oga* because they paid my papa—now I work here until he can pay them back." She patted me on the head. "I have been here for eight years. Your wounds will heal in less time than that."

"Oh my God. What about your mum?" I asked.

She lifted my emptied bowl and said, "I never had a mum, but you still have your father. Rest, Bisola. I will be right back."

I thought of Mother and Sister, and imagined they hugged when they finally met, and one or both of them shed tears, and each was busy pouring eleven years of stories into the other. It was, I decided, my sister's turn with Mother.

The following morning, I woke up shaking from seeing an airplane drop from the sky, and Mother crawling out of the flames to safety, only to be chased by a fleet of sirens. Ikuseghan brought the baby into the small bedroom. She handed me his bottle and placed him in my lap. "Feed him. I have to bathe."

I nodded.

She winked. "I left something for you in the cupboard."

"Thank you," I said.

When the baby fell asleep, I placed him on the bed and went into the kitchen. I opened the cupboard, expecting to find the hot *asaro* that scented the air. There was a covered bowl pressed near the back wall. I opened it. Ikuseghan's keys looked better than a heaping pile of yam porridge. I pushed the cast-iron bars apart. The girl I had become did not recoil when the gate cried itself shut. She raced down the stairs, through the muck of that arid garden, and ambled into the road.

ABOUT THE AUTHOR

KESHA AJOSE-FISHER WAS BORN in Chicago, raised in Lagos, Nigeria, and returned to the United States with her family in the early nineties. She won the 2020 Ken Kesey Prize through the Oregon Book Awards for her debut collection: *No God Like the Mother*. She is also an Oregon Literary Fellow and a relentless student of the human condition. Ajose-Fisher's work has appeared in collections such as *The Alchemy, The Phoenix, The Buckman Journal*, and was recently anthologized in *Dispatches from Anarres: Tales in Tribute to Ursula K. Le Guin*.

ACKNOWLEDGMENTS

I WOULD FIRST LIKE to thank my awesome husband, Kevin, for his unconditional love and devotion, and for his silence when I am writing. Next, I owe a huge thank you to my dog, Oscar, for reading my first drafts, for loving me even after discovering my addiction to commas, and for the noise-cancelling headphones.

To my beautiful babies: Omo'dara, thank you for creating the art for the cover. You are incredibly talented and absolutely deserving of all the good the world has to offer. To Omo'lara, thanks for cheering me on through big and little successes. You are smart, kind, and the best laughing buddy there is. To Ryanne, thanks for being easy to parent and for your curious and independent spirit. The world has no idea what you have in store for it. To Declan, my one and only son, thanks for finding the happy in each moment, for your willingness to meditate with me, and for our singing and rapping sessions during car rides. I love you all so much.

To the RASKS crew—my brothers, Sunny Ajọsẹ and Richard Johnson Ajọsẹ—thanks for teaching me to be strong in a world set to devour my kind of softness. To my sister, Angela Akinde, thanks for never missing an opportunity to keep me grounded. If you ever say a nice thing to me, I'll know I have lost you. Your kind of honesty is rare, and I am fortunate to have you. To Dad, Mr. Akinsanya Sunny Ajọsẹ, thank you for being gentle with me over the years, and for teaching me to write. You always made me feel like a princess. To Ma, Sheila Nadine Ajọsẹ, gone too soon but ever present—you deserved a better run at this life. Because of you, I walk with my head high, find humor in the darkest of places, and love dogs beyond what some might consider normal.

To Mrs. Mori, thank you for encouraging me to tell my stories my way, for introducing me to authors who continue to inspire me, and for lifting me up when I nearly fell to bits. May your soul rest in peace. To Ms. Simms, thank you for allowing me to create whole worlds—no matter how ludicrous—out of words. I am forever indebted to you for your kindness—even when I was no longer your student. You and Mrs. Mori are the kind of teachers every child deserves.

To Sandra Kapsiotis, thank you for dragging me out of immaturity. Because of you, I survived. To Carla D. Lett, Amee Ochoa Bonson—thanks for making my time at Lincoln so much more enjoyable.

Thank you to all the women who stepped in to raise me, and to those in my sisterhood—you know who you are.

My love to the Ajọsẹ and the Johnson families.

Dick and Jane Fisher, thank you for raising a wonderful man for me to call my husband. I thank you for loving my children, for your willingness to read my work, and for the encouragement to move forward.

To my fellow writers who have built me up, or torn me down only to build me up again, thank you for all the support, and for the many, many, many years of reading the stuff that came out of my head. Ginille Hayden Forest, Kelli Anderson, Angela Tipton, Phillip Englund, and Dr. Rita Carey (RIP).

To my first editor, Andrew Durkin, thanks for your patience.

To my agent, Kate Garrick, thank you for all your guidance. To Laura Stanfill and Forest Avenue Press, thank you for a second chance at keeping this book alive in a way I never expected was possible. To Gigi Little, the new cover is as my daughter says, "Fire!"

To Joanna Harrison, you were right, it is all happening. Thank you for how you always show up.

Thank you to all the amazing and talented authors who shared a blurb or review. We're family now.

To Literary Arts and the Oregon Book Awards, you have opened doors to rooms I did not believe I belonged in. For this, I am grateful.

I appreciate the roles you all have played in my life. Your lessons are blessings.

Be well, everyone.

Love, K.

NO
GOD
LIKE THE
MOTHER
Readers' Guide

GLOSSARY

Nigerian pidgin or broken English is derived from British English. It is used in informal conversations, or when people from different dialects need to communicate with each other.

The particle *dey* is the equivalent of the English word *there*, and is used to mark verbs for present tense and progressive aspect. *Nah* means *is*, and *wetin* means *what*. An example of these together is *"Nah wetin dey* do you?" This means: "What is bothering you?"

Sometimes words are deliberately repeated, as we see in "I go go market," which means "I will go to the market"; whereas, if one says, "I *go* market," it means, "I went to the market."

A short glossary of pidgin in this book:

a fi okunbo: we came through the river
abeg: I beg or please
abuhshun: abortion
adupe: giving thanks
ah ahn: ugh
am/im: him/her/it
amuti: drunkard
Assalamumalaikum: a traditional greeting among Muslims: peace be upon you
beni: yes and 'that's how it is'
bosita: get out
bu onje fun: get her some food
chop: eat
commot: get out
dash: give
dem: they
dey: there
dis: this
eba: a sour and starchy vegetable food made from dried and grated cassava (*garri*)

ehn: yes, what, or aha; sometimes used to emphasize a statement

ehn ehn: no

ejo: please

Fajr: a Muslim prayer offered to God at dawn

Fela Kuti: pioneer of Nigeria's Afrobeat music

igbo: marijuana

kuttas: quarters, as in 'boy's quarters'

mah/sah: used out of respect for an older person, i.e. ma'am or sir

nah: is

nko: what about…

o: an expression used to emphasize the end of one's statement

oku: the dead, a corpse

pele (or *e pele*): an apology

sef: also

sharrap: shut up

shay: will you

so gbo: you hear?

suru (*E ni suru*): have patience

thin: thing

Toub: a traditional piece of long clothing worn by Sudanese
    women, wrapped around the body and over the head

wahala: trouble

wan: want

wetin: what

wit: with

AUTHOR'S NOTE

ORISA BI IYA KOSI is the Yoruba translation for *There is no God like the mother.* This phrase has appeared in songs and poems for as long as I can remember; but most remarkably when I first heard it sung at a funeral by a friend who had lost his mother. This revelation to me as a child, hearing mothers compared to God, burrowed itself profoundly within my soul. I spent much of my childhood in Lagos, Nigeria where I considered women to be the true heroes in life for their ability to keep the world turning amid so much chaos. When I chose to tell stories about the relationships between mothers and their children, particularly, their daughters, I knew immediately how to pay homage to every single woman who passed through my life: *Orisa Bi Iya Kosi.*

A TRIBUTE TO TWO TEACHERS

SOMETIMES WHEN A PERSON enters your life, it is only in their absence that you learn to appreciate their existence. Three years into living in America, my world capsized. My mother went away, Father was too far away, and I found myself sinking into despair. Salvation came at the hands of an aunt in the Bay Area. She was a single mother with two children still at home, and I entered as a third: to be fed, to be clothed, to be reared—broken as I was. Piecing together another person's fragmented project is hard work, a constant reassessing of one's physical and mental effort; this, I know now.

Also difficult is being the child within that equation, born faultlessly into conditions that required steady footing, even as my world continuously fell apart.

My only safe space was in between the pages of my journal. In my junior year, I met Mrs. Mori. She was an English teacher who encouraged me to write stories about Nigeria. I dug deep and hauled out tales grounded in superstition—with witches and spirits and *juju* (voodoo)—as I had heard it used to control the world around us. After she read my feeble attempt at weaving a supernatural world through realistic fiction, Mrs. Mori pulled me aside and drew down the walls I had in place by telling me that I was a phenomenal writer.

Me?

While staggering through this compliment—and I'm still shocked whenever anyone likes my work—I heard her say, "With your talent, a bit more guidance will take you far." She then suggested I read Ursula K. Le Guin's work, and gave me a copy of *The Left Hand of Darkness*. "What you want to do with storytelling is possible," she told me, "and here is someone who does it well."

Granted, I do not write science fiction, but I did learn from Le Guin that it was possible to create new worlds from nothing and escape the real one anytime I chose.

Years later, my writing was included in the   anthology *Dispatches from Anarres: Tales in Tribute to Ursula K. Le Guin* (Forest Avenue Press).

I wrote "Mr. Uncle's Favor," a simple story about friendship through the eyes of a child determined to alter her world. Being included in that anthology was a full-circle moment for me in my writing career. I did not realize what kind of friend I had earned in Mrs. Mori until I revisited our time together when I shared my connection to Le Guin. After that story was accepted, I wrote a brief note about my first experience with Le Guin's work.

"Mrs. Mori was the sort of teacher every child deserves for her persistent patience and unwavering kindness," I had written.

Left unsaid in that brief tribute was that by the time I became a senior at Albany High, I was on my own, at times living with friends and sometimes wherever space was made for me on a stranger's couch or floor. Mrs. Mori was not my teacher that year, but our friendship remained. I often stopped by her classroom to say hello and to update her on my life. She would hand me an apple or half her meal, and I imagine now, she knew it was likely the only thing I had to eat some days. She and Ms. Simms (another beautiful soul in the form of a teacher in my life) helped me look for safe housing and guided me through that difficult final year of high school. Even with more chaos than love in my life, I was determined to graduate with my head held high. As a graduation gift, both women took me to purchase a dress and shoes to wear for the ceremony. No one in my family attended, but I always remember those women cheering as I crossed the threshold into my future. For that act and many more, these teachers reshaped my perspective on humanity then, and still.

I only wish Mrs. Mori were here with us to see how a moment of lifting me up changed my life.

I have not seen or heard from Ms. Simms in many years. I hope our paths cross again in this life.

I wanted to honor these teachers for showing up for the work required outside of the classroom. Because of them, I believe that when we lift up our girls, the world is rewarded with strong women. I'll carry my teachers' benevolence with me always.

BOOK CLUB QUESTIONS

1. The relationships between mothers and children by birth or by proxy are present throughout this collection. In the title story, "No God Like the Mother," how does Ayomide's discovery of who Iya'agba is affect the way Ayomide walks through the rest of her journey? What is the meaning of Tokunbo?

2. Marley, the protagonist in "Sleep," does not name her husband and children until late in the story. Is there any significance to this? What are some parallels between her feelings about her loss and her blackness in Portland, Oregon? Is Marley alive by the end?

3. In "The Silence Between Us," why is the relationship between Emilola and Kareem so complicated? Who does Fatima become to Emilola? What was Emilola and Fatima's expectation during the drive? What do you think happens?

4. In what way is setting important to each story?

5. During an assault, in "Thief," Lynn can only think of what her mother will say. Why is that? How does it connect to the overarching themes of the collection? What kind of a person is Pierre? Does his story deserve to be examined? Why or why not?

6. Why does "The Bride Price" begin with a celebration? What are your thoughts on authors telling stories from an outsider's perspective?

7. Which is your favorite story and why?

8. The characters in these stories often find themselves in conflict with traditional values and or practices. Why do you think the author chose to focus on this distinctly human condition?

9. In "Snow by Morning," why are some of the characters nameless? How does the housegirl having two names inform your response to the question? How does Bisola

cope with her mother's absence? Why does she rely on her dreams when processing the world around her? What is the significance of the Islamic prayers? What kind of women do Oge and Bisola have the potential of becoming based on their time together?

10. The relationship between Aduke and her aunt is dysfunctional, in "In Her Shoes," yet they manage to live together peacefully. What are your thoughts on this arrangement? How does this affect the way each processes the loss of a family member? What do you observe about the aunt and her role in Aduke's life—as Nigerians and in their interactions as Nigerians living in America?

11. Jonnie and Margaret, in "No More Trouble," seemed to seek out the potential for love even without ever knowing it. Is it naive for young lovers to want something they have never known? Is the relationship doomed because of their ages? How will Margaret's decision affect the relationship if Jonnie discovers it? Who do they become if life allows them to stay and grow together?

12. What is the significance of the book's title?

13. Consider Josephine's view of motherhood in "Nobody's Child." What is her view of sex based on her upbringing? What is her view of herself when she discovers the flaw in her mind's processing of her experience? Why has Josephine chosen to keep her truth from her daughter? How would the truth have affected their relationship? Is the relationship between Josephine and her mother rectifiable?

14. Are there any characters who you were sad to say goodbye to or whose stories you feel aren't quite finished yet?